I0561037

Joseph S. Taylor

A Romance of Providence

Joseph S. Taylor

A Romance of Providence

ISBN/EAN: 9783337348595

Printed in Europe, USA, Canada, Australia, Japan

Cover: Foto ©Andreas Hilbeck / pixelio.de

More available books at **www.hansebooks.com**

A

ROMANCE OF PROVIDENCE:

BEING

A HISTORY

OF THE

CHURCH OF THE STRANGERS,

IN THE CITY OF NEW YORK.

EDITED BY

JOSEPH S. TAYLOR.

NEW YORK:

WILBUR B. KETCHAM,

71 BIBLE HOUSE.

PREFACE.

AT the Monthly Meeting of the Church of the Strangers for the month of November, 1886, Hon. George W. Clarke, Ph.D., introduced a resolution providing for the appointment of a committee to prepare a Church History. He supported the resolution with the following remarks :

"*Mr. President, Brethren and Sisters :*

"At the regular meeting of the Advisory Council, November, 1886, for the admission of new members, one of the brethren made an observation to which all gave assent, viz. : —'That the story of the good way in which the Lord has led us should be told for the comfort and edification of Christians in struggling Churches. This remark led to the resolution before you.

"Brethren, the most marvelous fact in the history of the Church of the Strangers is that it *has* a history. Its existence, rapid growth, usefulness, and prosperity for twenty years, as an independent Christian Church, without pew rents—mark it as one of the wonders of the religious world.

"Would not every friend of the Church of the Strangers give something to know how God has made it so great a blessing—something to know the methods used in keeping for a score of years this gate of Heaven wide open to perishing souls?

" And would not Christians everywhere be encouraged in the work of the Master by being made acquainted with the rich spiritual fruits that have been gathered from what seemed at the outset a most unpromising field ?

" In short, do not the members of this Church owe it to the cause of Christ to make all needful provision for letting the light of the example of the Church of the Strangers *shine*, that others, seeing its good work, may be helped in their efforts to glorify our Father Who is in Heaven ?

" The Advisory Council hopes the resolution will receive your favorable consideration."

The resolution was adopted, and Mr. Joseph S. Taylor, Mr. Marion J. Verdery, and Miss Cecile Sturtevant were appointed a committee to prepare the history.

In writing this book they have drawn from many sources and employed many hands in addition to their own. The subscriber has edited the material, so as to make a connected and, he hopes, a consistent story.

The Church of the Strangers just *came*: it was not devised by any man. Dr. Deems positively affirms that *he* did not plan or devise it, and that he never discovered the man who did. He was not *called* by the Church, nor did he *call* the Church. We have endeavored to show how the people of all creeds, sections, and nationalities gathered about him ; and how Providence has used them and him to perform a special function. A Church so unique in character, begun under the divine guidance amid circumstances so peculiar—may we not call its history 'A Romance of Providence " ?

J. S. T.

CONTENTS.

I.

THE STRANGERS' SUNDAY HOME.

II.

"THE CHURCH OF THE STRANGERS." .

III.

A PRINCELY GIFT.

IV.

NEW QUARTERS.

V.

INTERNAL ECONOMY.

viii   *CONTENTS.*

XVII.

RECEPTION OF THE PASTOR.

Dr. Deems Sails for the East—Rev. Edward M. Deems Becomes Tem-
porary Pastor—A Reception Committee—Address by Joseph J.
Little, Esq.—Reply by Dr. Deems—Dr. Clarke's Address to Rev.
E. M. Deems—Rev. E. M. Deems's Reply.....................

XVIII.

" HOW " AND " WHY."

Prefatory—From a Jeweler—A Young Man—A Widow—A Young
Scotchman—Another Young Man—The Father of the Above—A
Widow—A Trustee—A Business Man—An Artist—A Publisher—
A Professional Man—A Young Woman—A Former Member of the
Advisory Council—An Andover Theological Student............ 206

XIX.

WHAT THEN ?

What Is to Be the Future of the Church of the Strangers ?—Its Results
—Number of Members—Growth of Fraternal Feeling—North and
South—Every Church a Church of Strangers—Testimony of Dr.
Deems Quoted.................   229

XX.

SERMON BY DR. DEEMS........................... 238

ILLUSTRATIONS.

CHURCH OF THE STRANGERS...........................*Frontispiece.*
CHARLES F. DEEMS, D.D., LL.D............................... 14
COMMODORE VANDERBILT.. 26
MRS. FRANK A. VANDERBILT................................... 128
VANDERBILT MEMORIAL TABLET................................ 218

A ROMANCE OF PROVIDENCE

"The Strangers' Sunday Home."

"HISTORY," says Macaulay, " is a compound of poetry and philosophy." " Poetry," he says elsewhere, "is the art of employing words in such a manner as to produce an illusion on the imagination." The past, in short, is to be so painted on the canvas of history as to produce an illusive picture. Sir Walter Scott's historical novels, which combine the facts of history with the inventions of the imagination, and Macaulay's History of England, by whose magic the dead past lives again, both justify this view of historical writing. In this book no pretension is made to reach any high ideal, save that of fidelity to truth; yet it is believed that there are passages in the following pages which justify the metaphorical title selected for the volume.

There *are* romances of Providence. Perhaps one of them can be found in the history of the Church of the Strangers.

Our Civil War closed by the surrender of the Con-
federate forces under General Lee, to the Federal
forces under General Grant, in April, 1865. At that
time there was a clergyman of the Southern Methodist Episcopal Church in North Carolina, who, born
in Maryland, had been educated in Pennsylvania,
married to a New York lady in New Jersey; and
had spent all his life from twenty years of age in
North Carolina   There he had been General Agent
for the American Bible Society, Professor in the State
University, and President of the Greensboro Female
College, which had greatly flourished under his ad-
ministration.   These positions naturally made him
well acquainted with the whole State, and created for
him friends in every circle. He had been honored
by his church with every ecclesiastical position in its
gift, except that of bishop, and had been spoken of
for the episcopacy.   In the discussion which brought
on the War, he opposed the secession of his State;
but when North Carolina seceded, after Virginia
had withdrawn from the Union, he was loyal to the
government which had been established, and he did
all he could for the Confederacy; when that succumbed, he immediately employed the advantages of
his position for reconstruction in Church and State.

In the progress of the War the Federal Government had sequestrated all the debts due citizens of
the United States by persons living in the Confed-
erate States.   The latter instituted a similar process.
In the year before the War, Dr. Deems had spent
six months in Europe, and in that time the person

whom he had left in charge of his affairs in North
Carolina had contracted debts in the North. When
called upon, Dr. Deems made a sworn statement of
the items of his indebtedness to New York merchants,
and at the same time said that if ever the War
closed he would repay this amount to his Northern
creditors. During the summer following General
Lee's surrender, Dr. Deems went to New York to
arrange for the payment of these debts. From this
stand-point he was able calmly to examine the position in which he stood at home. He had four children ; North Carolina was impoverished ; the people
were his friends; but he saw little prospect of doing
them good, or of educating his children; while
he would be a burden on a church that had been ter-
ribly crippled by the War. In early life, Dr. Deems
had preached a winter in New York, and made many
friends. Some still felt kindly towards him. It was
believed that he could employ his talents in editing
a paper which might go far toward bringing about a
good state of feelings between the sections, and at
the same time support his family and educate his
children. It was in this view that he at last concluded to undertake such an enterprise. He returned
to North Carolina and obtained about $600 in sub-
scription to the new weekly, which was to be called
The Watchman.

It was a bold undertaking. The paper was to
appear weekly, and to be about the size of the *New
York Observer.* Dr. Deems hired a small room at
119 Nassau Street, and made an engagement with

Messrs. Gray & Green, printers, corner of Frankfort
and Jacob Streets, to do his printing ; while he and
his son, now Dr. Frank M. Deems, did all the editing, correspondence, book-keeping, and mailing. The
first number cost half the amount he had brought
with him from North Carolina, and he had engaged
to supply several hundred subscribers with the paper
for one year. He had on him that burden, with a
family of five persons to support. The first number
of *The Watchman* appeared the First of January,
1866, and fifty-two numbers were brought out. Dr.
Deems has recently said to a friend ; " No one can
ever know the agony I endured through that year. I
had not learned the domestic economies of the city
at that time, but did everything at the highest price.
I was compelled to edit the paper and obtain subscriptions and advertisements enough to meet the
weekly demand of my printers and of my family. I
had no office which I could occupy at night, and so
used to spend my evenings in the billiard room of
French's Hotel, opposite the *Sun* office. There was
warmth there, and I got so used to writing to the
click of the billiard balls, that when I changed I
really came to miss their annotating sounds."

In making his calculations for the success of *The
Watchman*, it was very natural for Dr. Deems to
suppose that upon reconstruction, all the mail service
would be rehabilitated.. This opinion he shared with
a very large majority of thoughtful men of every
part of the country. Those who recollect that year
will remember it as one of the blackest in the annals

of this country. The conflict between President
Johnson and Congress disturbed every thing, and
acrimonious conflicts retarded the reconstruction of
the country. The mails throughout the South were
in a most deplorable condition. In some places
people would be three weeks in getting papers that
had been mailed in New York. Hoping and toiling,
Dr. Deems went forward ; but throughout the whole
year he was coming more and more to the conclusion
that the state of the country was such that, without
capital, it would be impossible to maintain so large a
weekly paper until the times should grow propitious.
In one year from its beginning, *The Watchman*
ceased. From the time that Dr. Deems saw it was
going to close, he laid aside the subscriptions which
came in and returned them to the subscribers whose
time he could not fill out. This scrupulousness,
naturally, made it harder for him to live. When it
is learned that he conducted it so long on such principles, without one dollar of capital and any outside
help, immediately after a long War, in which he had
been on the losing side, and had conducted it among
a people who had been on the opposite side ; and
when it is further known that he created a debt of
only $2,000, it must be admitted that the opinion of
the late James Harper, one of the founders of the
house of Harper Brothers, was correct—that it was
"the greatest feat of publication ever achieved in
New York."

It was amid his terrific struggles with *The Watchman* that the first steps were made which led towards

the "Church of the Strangers." It will be remembered that Dr. Deems was a clergyman of the Methodist Episcopal Church South, still in such good standing there as to have been elected by his Conference to the General Conference of his church, which was held in New Orleans in April, 1866, at which a number of votes were cast for him as Bishop. This Conference took him one month from his work on *The Watchman.* He had no ecclesiastical associations in New York; the differences between the Northern and the Southern Methodist Churches never were so great, the feelings never so bitter. Dr. Deems had been in the Confederacy through the whole fight, and, as he once said, walked the streets of New York and engaged in his daily work with the weight of Andersonville prison around his neck. Neither his own family nor Southern people coming to purchase goods could attend church in New York; for almost everywhere the pulpit resounded with denunciations of "rebels" and the "rebellion," and the voice of the Gospel seemed hushed in the land. Dr. Deems relates that every Sunday through the winter and spring he had received a lashing in church. One Sunday afternoon, as he was then boarding in 15th Street, he went to St. George's Church, of which the senior Dr. Tyng was rector. He was very tired, having worked hard during the week. The sexton refused to show him a seat; he must wait till the pewholders were in. He stood twenty minutes, until he became so weary that he was compelled to return to his room without having the comfort of the

service. He said that that made him determined if
ever he had rule in a church, no man should have to
stand one minute who came in one minute before
the service opened. Now, 1887, St. George's is a free
church, free to all strangers.

Invitations to deliver addresses began to reach the
Doctor. The American Bible Society, which had
sent him as its General Agent to North Carolina,
asked him to make a speech at its anniversary; this
called attention to him afresh. There were noble
Christians who rose above sectional strife and acknowledged Christianity wherever they saw its fruits.

On Sunday, July 15, 1866, Dr. Deems was invited
to preach a sermon before the Young Men's Christian
Association of the Hedding Methodist Episcopal
Church in Jersey City. Among those who were present was the wife of Mr. Frerichs, the artist. That
lady had known the Doctor when he was President of
the College in Greensboro, N. C.; but had not seen
him for years. After hearing this sermon she followed
him to the house where he was dining, and accompanied
him to the ferry-boat, and employed the time with im-
portunities that he should begin preaching regularly in
New York. His replies, that there was no church of
his denomination in the city; that there would be no
propriety in attempting to establish a Southern Methodist Church; that he was making a violent effort to
support his family, and pay his debts; seemed to make
no impression upon her. She spoke as if she regarded
herself a prophetess sent to direct a servant of the
Lord. As they parted she concluded her appeal by

saying: "I am very sure that God intends you to preach in New York. I do beg of you to promise me that you will preach just four weeks somewhere in New York, even if it's in a garret, or a cellar, or a tub!" The promise was extorted that an effort would be made to gratify her desire.

In accordance with this promise, next day Dr. Deems went to the University on Washington Square (of which institution he is now one of the Councilors) to see what he could do. He had seen the announcement of some preaching there. Upon his arrival he found a quiet, meek-mannered little janitor. The Doctor asked him if a place for preaching could be hired in the University. "For whom?" inquired the janitor, inspecting the Doctor from head to foot. "For me," was the reply. "No," said the janitor; "we have no place to suit *you.*" This janitor died shortly after, and Dr. Deems never became well enough acquainted with him to ask what he meant by stating that there was no place that would suit *him.* It appeared that while the eloquent Rev. Dr. Hawks was occupying the large chapel of the University, an eccentric preacher was holding forth every Sunday afternoon in the smaller chapel, and that the latter apartment could be obtained for morning service, at $25 a month. That seemed to be within his reach ; at any rate, he determined to give, out of his poverty, that much to the Lord. On Saturday, July 21st, he put this notice in the *New York Herald :* "The Rev. Dr. Deems, of North Carolina, will preach in the chapel of the University to-morrow at 11 o'clock." On Sunday, July 22, 1866, he repaired to the chapel, where he had to be his own sexton and precentor, and employed in the service such hymns as everybody knew, for there were no books. The congregation consisted of sixteen persons. The persons not of the preacher's family were, it is believed, the following: Mr. W. H. Chase, Mr. Clement Disosway, Mrs. and Miss Frerichs, Mr. Nehemiah Pratt, Gen. Richardson, of Tennessee; J. M. Roberts, Dr. N. W. Seat, Mr. S. T. Taylor, Mrs. Mary E. Tucker, Mr. W. J. Woodward, Mr. A. C. Worth. [Six are dead, 1886.] The text was, " Philip went down to the city of Samaria and preached Christ unto them." At the conclusion of the service it was announced that the Doctor would preach on the next Sunday, and on the following Saturday the announcement was repeated in the *Herald.* On Sunday, the 29th, there were over thirty persons present. On Sunday, August 5th, there were over seventy persons present. As the preacher's promise did not bind him beyond the month, and as he saw no way of continuing this work, he announced at the close of the service, that for three weeks he had enjoyed Paul's pleasure of preaching in his own hired house, but that Paul must have found tent-making in the East more profitable than the preacher found journalism in the West, and that consequently the next Sunday would close this series of sermons, as he could not afford to preach for nothing and supply a place for service. A large number of those who had been attracted to the service were Southerners. One of them, Gen. Richardson, of Ten-

nessee, asked the Doctor whether, if a place were provided, he would continue to preach; and the reply
was, that the preacher's Sundays were wholly unoc-
cupied and he would willingly preach for those who
desired to hear him. Whereupon it was proposed that
a collection be taken up, and that Dr. Deems be requested to continue preaching. · The collection a little
more than paid the month's rent. On the following
Sunday, the 12th of August, the chapel was packed;
there had dropped in many whose churches were
closed. It was then proposed that there be some
regular organization to afford a free place of worship
for strangers from all parts of the world, who might
be in the city.

At the close of the service it was resolved to form
an executive committee of gentlemen of different denominations to provide for keeping the place open for
worship. They had the following card printed, to be
distributed through the congregation and around the
neighborhood :—

"THE STRANGERS' SUNDAY HOME.—In the Chapel
of the University, Washington Square, New York,
under the pastoral care of the Rev. Dr. Deems, of
North Carolina, there is a congregation composed of
members of the different denominations of Christians.
Divine service is conducted every Sunday, and no dis-
tinction of sectarianism is allowed. The worship of
God is the simple objèct of the assemblage. It is
specially designed for strangers who visit the city and
particular pastoral oversight of the young men who
have recently engaged in business in New York. A

Sunday-School assembles at 9 o'clock, and the public service begins punctually at 10½ o'clock. *The Seats are Free.* All are cordially invited. Visitors to the city, if sick or needing a pastor, can have the services of Rev. Dr. Deems, whose residence for the present is ———.

" This enterprise is maintained wholly by voluntary contributions. You are respectfully requested to assist us. We solicit donations or weekly subscriptions. If you are residing in the city, please say how much you will pay weekly, and on Sunday deposit your contribution in the basket, in an envelope, with your name upon it, so that you may be duly credited. The Executive Committee are: Major C. L. Nelson, 23 East 37th Street; Dr. Gardner (of Evans, Gardner & Co.), 380 Broadway; Col. B. B. Lewis (of Lewis, Daniel & Co.), 21 Nassau Street; S. T. Taylor, 349 Canal Street; Dr. Seat, 23 West 31st Street; J. M. Roberts (of Ring, Ross & Roberts), 86 Front Street; K. M. Murchison, 188 Front Street; Dr. F. M. Garrett (of Garrett, Young & Co.), 33 Warren Street; R. C. Daniel (of Lewis, Daniel & Co.), 21 Nassau Street; and J. L. Gaines (of Harris, Gaines & Co.), 15 Whitehall Street."

It will be observed that the Pastor's residence was left in blank; the income was so small and he was so compelled to study small economies that he had to look out for the cheapest boarding-place in which he and his family could live in any degree of respectability. It is proper to add that a Sunday-School was formed in the very beginning, and put into the charge of Mr. R. C. Daniel, of Kentucky, of the firm of Lewis, Daniel & Co., then brokers in Wall Street.

The large chapel of the University was a much more commodious apartment than the little chapel in which we worshiped. It was very beautiful. It has since been cut up into rooms for office purposes. At that time it was occupied by a Protestant Episcopal congregation, in charge of the Rev. Dr. Francis L. Hawks. Dr. Hawks was a North Carolinian, and had distinguished himself at the bar in his own State before he entered the Episcopal Ministry. He had been rector of the old St. Thomas Church, when it stood at the corner of Broadway and Houston Street. He was magnificently gifted ; a man of great natural eloquence, of varied learning, and of surprising powers of elocution. During the Civil War he had some trouble in New York, and had gone to New Orleans. On his return to New York his friends rallied about him and were preparing to build him a new church, the nucleus of which was then the congregation of the large chapel of the University. Dr. Hawks died on the 26th of September, 1866. In his last illness he frequently sent for Dr. Deems. They had both recently been elected to Chairs in the University of North Carolina, and had both declined. In one of the latest interviews between the two gentlemen, Dr. Hawks said to a friend that his chief ambition had been disappointed ; that for years it had been his desire to be president of the University of North Carolina, and have Dr. Deems as his lieutenant, in the assurance that they two could make the University

one of the greatest institutions in the country. He
once said: " Dr. Deems, three times I have been
offered the mitre, and three times have I put it aside.
Never let your Church make you bishop. God has
some better thing for you. Your calling is to preach
Christ, Christ crucified. Pursue that steadily and have
no doubt that God will give you great success in this
great city."

II.

1867-1868.

"The Church of the Strangers."

THE year 1867 was a struggle for existence. Upon the death of Dr. Hawks negotiations were made for the occupancy of the large chapel; but the "Strangers' Sunday Home" could not be removed till the first Sunday in May, 1867. Its accommodations were then increased four fold, but it was still a mere assembly without church organization.

In the autumn of 1867, many persons expecting to remain in the city, some a longer, some a shorter time, some perhaps permanently, came to Dr. Deems offering their church letters; but there was no " Church." These repeated offers led to much thought and prayer; consultation also was had with the authority of the Church of which Dr. Deems was then a minister, and with other godly and learned persons. The result was a determination to organize, in the City of New York, a free, independent church of Jesus Christ. On the last two Sundays in December, 1867, it was publicly announced that on the first Sunday in January, 1868, such a Church would be organized. The following was the paper read by Dr. Deems:—

" It is probably known to all present that I am a

Charles F. Deeny

minister of the Gospel in good and regular standing in the Methodist Episcopal Church, South, and a member in particular of the North Carolina Annual Conference.

"In July, 1866, at the urgent request of Christian people of several denominations, I began preaching in the University of this city. At their urgency these services were continued until a congregation was formed of many who hold this as their regular place of worship, and of many others who are in occasional or very frequent attendance. The wants of many strangers visiting New York, and of many residents whose ecclesiastical connections have not been permanently formed, seem to demand the existence of such an institution. So strong is the conviction of intelligent and devout people that such an undertaking should be persevered in, that they united in a request to the Bishops of the Church of which I am a clergyman, that I might be returned as Pastor of this flock which God's providence has seemed to commit to my charge. In accordance with this expressed wish the Bishops, at their Annual Meeting, directed me to remain, and in accordance with that action the Bishop presiding at the session of my Conference, lately held, has appointed me to this work.

"That all things may be done decently and in order, as the Apostle Paul directs, it appears to be necessary that some organization be made which shall give us a place among the churches of Jesus Christ. All of you who are communicants naturally desire to be acknowledged as regular members of the Church Militant, and that when Providential circumstances indicate the necessity of removal, you may be able to bear with you the evidence of having been orderly disciples of Christ, and under Christian pastoral direction.

"In the XIXth Article of the Church of England, and in the XIIIth Article of the 'Articles of Religion' of the Church of which I am a minister, it is set forth that—'The visible Church of Christ is a congregation of faithful men, in which the pure Word of God is preached and the Sacraments duly administered according to Christ's ordinance in all those things that of necessity are requisite to the same.'

"In the preface to the Book of Common Prayer of the Protestant Episcopal Church in the United States of America, it is said that—'It is a most invaluable part of that blessed *liberty wherewith Christ hath made us free*, that in this worship different forms and usages may, without offense, be allowed, provided the substance of the Faith be kept entire: and that in every Church what cannot be clearly determined to belong to doctrine must be referred to Discipline, and therefore, by common consent and authority, may be altered, abridged, enlarged, amended, or otherwise disposed of as may seem most convenient for the edification of the people according to various exigencies of times and occasions.'

"In its 'Form of Government,' Chapter II., Section IV., published with its 'Confession of Faith,' the Presbyterian Church in the United States of America sets forth that—'A particular church consists of a number of Professing Christians with their offspring, voluntarily associated together for divine worship and godly living, agreeably to the Holy Scriptures, and submitting to a certain form of government.'

" Christianity exists *subjectively* in the rule of Christ in simple individuals, *objectively* as an ' organized visible society, as a kingdom of Christ on Earth, as a Church.' ' The word church like the Scotch *kirk*, the German *kirche*, the Swedish *kyrkc*, and like terms in the Slavonic languages, must be derived through the Gothic, from the Greek κυρίακον, *i c.*, belonging to the Lord. It may signify the material house of God, or the local congregation, or, in the complex sense, the organic unity of all believers.'

" Believing these to be correct statements of the truth as touching this matter in the liberty where-with Christ has made us free, in the fear of God, and that, for your edification the Gospel may be preached and the sacraments duly administered and orderly dis-cipline maintained, it is proposed that all who are like-minded do form themselves into a congregation of Christian people, of which I am to be the Pastor so long as the Providence of God and the authorities of my own branch of Christ's Church shall continue me in this special office and ministry.

" That I may surely know who are minded to be thus under my pastoral charge, I shall, if God will, on the next Lord's day, being the first Sunday in Janu-ary, A.D., 1868, receive into this Society all the fol-lowing persons, to wit:

" (1) Such as present letters showing their good stand-in any branch of God's visible Church ; (2) such as declare that they have so been and desire so now to be, but by reason of circumstances which they could not control are not able to present letters of membership; and (3) such as desire to join upon their sincere and hearty profession of faith in that statement of Christian Doctrines commonly known as the 'Apostles' Creed,' and of an earnest 'desire to flee from the wrath to come and to be saved from their sins.'

"It is understood (1) that all such applicants have been baptized or desire to receive Christian baptism, in such mode as they may of conscience elect, by sprinkling, pouring, or immersion; (2) that all things thereafter necessary for the proper ordering of the things which Christ hath appointed to His church, shall, so far as this congregation of faithful people may be concerned, be by them determined 'according to the various exigencies of times and occasions;' (3) that nothing hereby or herein done shall be considered as affecting the relations to any branch of Christ's Church now held by any, except so far as they themselves shall choose, nor as in any way or degree touching the ecclesiastical relations of the Pastor, or as modifying the present position or relations of such pew-holders in this chapel,* or other attendants upon the ministry in this congregation as may not feel perfectly free to enter this Christian Society.

" Wherefore, as many as desire to avail themselves of the benefit of this organization will present themselves on the next Lord's day at the Holy Com-

---

* This alludes to a few persons to whom, by special arrangement, pews had been let by the Committee.

munion, that their names may be taken and registered as members of the Christian Society to be known for the present by the name which in the past has distinguished it, 'The Church of the Strangers.' "

On the fifth day of January, 1868, the following thirty-two persons enrolled themselves according to the terms in the above paper, and formed themselves into the " Church of the Strangers ; " whereupon the sacrament of the Lord's Supper was administered :

Mrs. Amelia E. Backett, Miss Susan Backett (Mrs. Potter), Mrs. Mary Brown, Mrs. Mary Day, Mrs. Anna D. Deems, Francis M. Deems, Miss Mary L.Deems (Mrs. Verdery), Edward M. Deems (Pastor Westminster Church, New York), Miss Catherine Dewitt, Mrs. Clara Frerichs, Mrs. Mary F. Gillespie, Miss Cordelia Gillespie (Mrs. Bermingham`, Wm. S. Harper, Mrs. Mary F. Horne, Mr. N. J. W. LeCato, Mr. B. B. Lewis, Mrs. Juliet Lewis, Mrs. Hannah L. Lloyd, Mr. John McNair, Mrs. Lydia A. Massey, Mrs. Annie McDonald, Mr. Charles L. Nelson, Mrs. Henrietta S. Nelson, Prof. Charles S. Stone (Cooper Union), Mrs. Helen O. Stone, Miss Cecile Sturtevant, Mr. Samuel T. Taylor, Mr. Eugene Thumm, Gen. John C. Vaughan, Mr. Wm. J. Woodward, Mrs. Sallie K. Woodward, Rev. James Young. Of these thirty-two, there are now living—March, 1887—seventeen persons.

III.

1869-1870.

A Princely Gift.

" For he loveth our nation, and hath built us a synagogue."—LUKE, 7:5.

THE MERCER STREET CHURCH.

THE Mercer Street Church was organized by the Third Presbytery of New York, October 25, 1835, with twenty-eight members, coming from six different churches, but the great majority of them from the Laight Street Church, a branch of the Spring Street Church.

During the summer of 1834, a fine house of worship had been erected on Mercer Street, near Waverly Place, and the congregation went immediately into their new home. A call was given to Rev. Thomas H. Skinner, D.D., LL.D., at the time Professor of Sacred Rhetoric in Andover Theological Seminary. He accepted the call, and on November 11, 1835, was installed as first Pastor of the new Church. The congregation and membership grew rapidly in numbers and wealth, and at the end of Dr. Skinner's pastorate, February 17, 1848, there were over five hundred members on the roll. Dr. Skinner resigned to take the Professorship of Sacred Rhetoric, Pastoral Theology, and Church Government in Union Theological Seminary.

Rev. J. C. Stiles, D.D., LL.D , succeeded Dr. Skinner, and was installed June 8, 1848, coming from the Shockoe Hill, now Grace Street Church, Richmond, Va. Dr. Stiles' health failing him, he was compelled to resign his charge, which he did October 15, 1850. He accepted a general agency for the American Bible Society in the South, and subsequently occupied a pastorate in New Haven, Conn., and then took the lead in organizing the Southern Aid Society, to give support to feeble churches in the South. In his latest years he labored as an evangelist in Virginia, Alabama, Florida, Mississippi, Missouri, and Maryland.

Rev. Dr. George L. Prentiss became the third Pastor, and was installed April 30, 1851, resigning on account of ill health May 3, 1858. After two years spent abroad, Dr. Prentiss returned, and by earnest work gathered about him a new Church, now the Church of the Covenant, Rev. Dr. Marvin R. Vincent, present Pastor. He became Pastor of this Church in 1862, and resigned in 1873 to accept his present position as Professor of Pastoral Theology, etc., in Union Theological Seminary.

Rev. Dr. Walter Clarke was installed as Dr. Prentiss's successor in Mercer Street, February 16, 1859, and resigned December 26, 1860. He was succeeded by Rev. Dr. Russell Booth, who was Pastor when the property passed to the Church of the Strangers.

The whole number of persons admitted to membership in this Church was two thousand and twenty-six, of whom seven hundred and forty-nine made profession of faith, and twelve hundred and seventy-seven were received by certificate.

In 1869 the Mercer Street Presbyterian Church engaged lots from the Columbia College Corporation, on which to erect a church for themselves. The accomplishment of the latter object would throw their church on the market. But the proposed new church was never built. On the 16th day of September, 1870, the Presbytery of New York united the " Mercer Street Presbyterian Church " with the " First Presbyterian Church on University Place." By the terms of the union the new Church was called " The Presbyterian Church on University Place," and the Elders and Deacons of the former Churches became the Elders and Deacons of the new Church. Rev. Robert Russell Booth, D.D., who had been Pastor of the Mercer Street Church since 1861, was duly installed by the Presbytery on October 30, 1870, as Pastor of the Union Church.

In the meantime the Mercer Street Church had offered their property to Dr. Deems for $65,000, through his friend, the late Gen. James Lorimer Graham, who was a member of the University Place Presbyterian Church. Dr. Deems offered them $50,000 for the property. Their Pastor, Rev. Dr. Booth, said he would rather Dr. Deems should have it for $50,000 than any other person for $60,000.

An important Providential factor in the history of the Church of the Strangers must now be introduced. One Sunday, after service in the chapel of the University, two ladies were in attendance, who,

after the service, were introduced to Dr. Deems by
the Rev. Dr. Charles K. Marshall, of Vicksburg, as
" Mrs. Crawford and her daughter, of Mobile." These
ladies were visiting New York, and became interested
in Dr. Deems as a clergyman of their own denomination. The younger of these ladies, in the summer
of 1869, became the wife of the late Cornelius Vanderbilt. Mr. Vanderbilt's residence was on the block
next adjoining the University, but he never came to
the services in that chapel. In the days of his youth
Mr. Vanderbilt had received favors from the father of
Dr. Deems's wife, and had met the Doctor once
before the War, in 1860, and was so impressed with
what occurred at the interview that he repeated the
conversation a few days before he died. This com-
bination of circumstances, and the late acquaintance-
ship and a new wife to whom he was most sincerely
devoted, led the Commodore to regard the work for
the strangers with favor. He urged Dr. Deems to
visit him, and often catechized him closely as to his
views and plans. He admired the breadth of this
new religious society, and believed in the orthodoxy
of its Pastor.

The Commodore had never been a member of any
Church ; had been a very worldly and even profane
man ; but he had from his earliest childhood the
most unshaken faith in the Bible as the inspired
Word of God. He became impatient at any contra-
diction of this idea ; he regarded that man untrust-
worthy who did not receive the Bible as the Word of
God. Towards the close of life, when he was in

great agony, he expressed the fear that after his death it might be supposed that he had been influenced on that question by his friend and Pastor, and so he said to him : "Doctor, when I am gone I leave you to do justice to my memory. I want it known that I always believed the Bible, and on that subject you have had no more influence over me than this fan which I hold in my hand." Although he did become more attentive to religious matters and more devout before his death, yet at this period of our history he believed that there was such a thing as genuine religion, and that it was founded upon a belief in the Bible as the Word of God. Somehow he heard of the movement upon the part of the Mercer Street Presbyterian Church, and made up his mind to put it under the control of Dr. Deems. We cannot do better than to give the Doctor's account of the presentation in his own words, as reported in the *Homiletic Monthly*, of New York, July, 1880, and afterward republished in a London periodical, from which it is here reproduced :

"A short time before he started for the East, our reporter called on Rev. Dr. Deems to learn from him how he came in possession of the Church of the Strangers. The following is his account :

" Well, said he, the manual of the Church shows how I came to be preaching in New York in 1866. Before the organization of any Church, and while I was simply preaching to strangers, a lady of high character, living in Mobile, when on a visit to New York always attended our service with her daughter. With them

I became acquainted. The daughter was that excellent woman whom Commodore Vanderbilt had the
good fortune to make his second wife. I had very
slight personal acquaintance with the Commodore,
and had not seen him in six or seven years, so I supposed that I should probably not again meet my fair
hearers. I learned afterward that it had been intended that I should celebrate the marriage, and
that it would have been done but for my absence.
I also learned, after they had been married some
weeks and were living within a block of the place
where I was preaching, that there was a feeling that
I was neglecting them. I have never gone after rich
people, nor particularly avoided them; but when a
man, conspicuous for wealth or position, desires to
know me, he must always seek me. That was the
only thing that had kept me from visiting the Commodore and his new bride. But so soon as I discovered that it was expected, I called, and was very   •
warmly welcomed.

"The Commodore paid me special attention; we
conversed very freely, and I did not hesitate, when
it was proper, to introduce the subject of religion and
talk on it—I trust in a natural and proper way. On
all the visits the Commodore catechized me carefully
about my preaching, my past history and my expec-
tations of the future. He was always answered frankly.
One evening in the sitting-room the conversation ran
upon clerical beggars. I acknowledged that in early
life I had had some reputation in that line, but that I
deprecated the whole business. 'Now,' said I,

'here I am. Have been preaching two years almost within earshot of the Commodore. The rooms which I have occupied have been overrun with hearers. People have often said to me : " Why don't you see Mr. Lenox, or Mr. Stewart, or Mr. Astor, or Commodore Vanderbilt, and ask them to build you the church of the strangers? They ought to do it for the good of the city." And yet,' I added, ' the Commodore here will bear me witness that I have never solicited a dollar from him for any object on earth.' Touching his wife, he said : ' Frank, that is so ; the Doctor never has ; ' and gave a look at his wife as much as to say that he wished by that observation to raise me in her estimation. The look evidently said that it had raised me in his. And I added : ' And, Mrs. Vanderbilt, so long as there is breath in his body, I never shall.' Evidently he did not quite understand my remark, and changed his expression into one of those steely looks of his which were very piercing and very subduing ; but I never faltered—turning the whole thing off in a jocose manner, by saying : ' For, if he has lived to attain his present age and has not got the sense to see what I need and the grace to send it to me, he will die without the sight ! ' We all smiled at that, and the conversation changed.

"On a subsequent visit I met Daniel Drew at the house. It was shortly after one of the great financial battles between Commodore Vanderbilt and Mr. Drew. The lion and the tiger were lying down a little while together. Mr. Drew had repeatedly attended the service I was holding in the University chapel, and had

COMMODORE VANDERBILT.

echoed Mrs. Vanderbilt's earnest praises of the usefulness of our little congregation. The Commodore
catechised me closely as to my views of Christian work,
and I answered him to the best of my ability and with
frankness. About that time the Mercer Street Presbyterian Church had negotiated for lots uptown belonging to Columbia College, and had put their own
edifice upon the market. Its Pastor, Dr. Booth, had
always seemed friendly to me. My friend, James
Lorimer Graham, Esq., conversed with me about
purchasing it, and I had authorized him to offer $50,-
000. Somehow this had got to the Commodore's ears,
but I did not know it, and did not intend to ask him for
a cent. My impressions of his character at that time
were, at least, not favorable. I regarded him as an
unscrupulous gatherer of money, a man who aimed
at accumulating an immense fortune, and had no very
pious concern as to the means. The few interviews
I had had with him after his marriage had modified
my opinions of the man. I discovered fine points of
which I had no suspicion. But still I was a little
afraid of him.

"On this particular Monday evening of which I
speak, he walked to the sitting-room door with me, as
his wont was, and as I passed out he said : ' Doctor,
come and see me to-morrow night.'

" ' I can't, Commodore.'

" ' Why can't you ? ' said he, in the tone of a man
not accustomed to be refused.

" ' Because,' said I, ' there are a couple of boys from
the South here who have come to be clerks and they

have no friends, and I have asked them to my board-
ing-house to become acquainted with my family;
hoping by this social tie to bind them to a virtuous
course of living.'

" ' Well, then,' said he, 'come around the next
night.'

" ' I can't, Commodore,' was my reply.

" ' Why can't you ? '

" ' Because every Wednesday night I have a little
prayer-meeting in the Bible House, never more than
thirteen or fourteen, but almost invariably four or five
being present, and I can't disappoint them.'

" ' Well,' said he, ' come around Thursday night.'

" ' I can't, Commodore.'

" ' Why ? ' he asked with a good-natured growl.

" ' Because,' said I, ' I have engaged to marry a
couple of very poor people on the west side of the
town, and it would never do to disappoint them. You
know how that is yourself,' alluding to the fact of his
recent marriage, and of his not being able to find me
to perform his marriage ceremony.

" ' Well,' said he, pleasantly, ' Doctor, come when
you can.'

" Having pondered over the impressiveness and rep-
etition of his invitations, I concluded I would go on
the following Saturday evening, to make a call in ac-
knowledgment of his hospitality. It was about eight
o'clock. There were visitors. I sat about half an
hour conversing with the circle, when I arose to go,
telling the Commodore that on Saturday evening
ministers of the Gospel ought to be quiet in their

studies, preparing themselves for the pulpit, and that
I had simply called around to thank him for his kind
invitations on the preceding Monday. He invited
me into a little office adjoining his bedroom, and sat
down upon one side of the table and pointed me to a
seat on the other. He said: 'Doctor, what is this
about that Mercer Street property?'

"'Well,' said I, 'Commodore, only this: It is in
the market. They want $65,000 for it, and I vent-
ured to offer them $50,000. It is on leased ground,
and I think it is about worth that.'

"'Well,' said he, 'how much have you got toward
your $50,000?'

"I felt in my pocket and playfully said:

"'Well, sir, as near as I can judge, about seventy-
five or eighty cents.'

"'How do you expect to pay for it then?'

"'Well, Commodore, this is my thought about it.
I have been here preaching some little time. My
work seems to prosper. I shall propose to the Mercer
Street Presbyterian Church to let me have their
building for six months. I shall preach in it those six
months. I shall announce to the people of New York
that I wish to establish, on an unsectarian basis, a
free Church for all comers, especially for strangers in
the city—a Church that shall be evangelical and un-
denominational; and I shall appeal for the money in
large sums and small. Now, Commodore, if God
wants me to stay in New York and do this work to
which my heart seems to be inclined, the money will
come. If not, the Mercer Street brethren have only

lost the use of their property six months, and it will
have been employed in Christian work.   But I believe
the money will come and the Church go on.'

"He looked me straight in the eye, and said:

"'Doctor, I'll give you the church!'

"I was mad in a minute.   I had not been made
so angry since I reached New York.   I thought that
Commodore Vanderbilt desired to obtain that property for some railroad or other business purpose, or
for his estate—that he had some deep design, and
chose to put me forward, supposing that I was a
greenhorn of a parson from the pine forests of North
Carolina, and he could use me.   I fired up, and,
leaning upon the table, looked him straight in the
eye, and said: 'Commodore Vanderbilt, you don't
know me!   There is not any man in America rich
enough to have me for a chaplain.'   I shall never
forget the look he returned.   He had been accustomed to be solicited.   Here he was, making the
largest offer of charity he ever had made, and found
a man refusing to accept $50,000!   It was an amazed
and quizzical look.   It was the look of a man who
had a new sensation, and could not tell whether he
was enjoying it or not.   As soon as he could frame
a reply, he said: 'Doctor, I don't know what you
mean.   Me have a chaplain!   The Lord knows I've
got as little use for a chaplain as any other man you
ever saw.   I want to give you this church, and give
it to you only.   Now, will you take it?'

"I paused a moment, and felt that, perhaps, I had
made a mistake in the man, and then said:

"'Commodore, I should not like to be under so great a pecuniary obligation to any gentleman, that, when I had the guns of the Gospel directed against the breastworks of any particular sin, and should see his head rising above them, I should be tempted to suspend my fire, or change the range of my shot.'

"'Doctor,' said he, 'I would not give you a cent if I did not believe that you were so independent a man that you would preach the Gospel 'as honestly to one man as to another. Now, I believe that, and I want to give you the church.'

"After the discharge of the lightning of my anger, I felt that a sort of April shower was coming. My eyes were moistening. It seemed to me a wonderful Providence; and you know we always think it is a wonderful Providence if it runs with our ideas. I extended my hand and said, 'Commodore, if you give me that church for the Lord Jesus Christ, I'll most thankfully accept it.'

"'No,' said he; 'Doctor, I would not give it to you that way, because that would be professing to you a religious sentiment I do not feel. I want to give you a church. That's all there is. It is one friend doing something for another friend. Now, if you take it that way, I'll give it to you.'

"We both rose at the same moment, and I took his hand and I said: 'Commodore, in whatever spirit you give it, I am deeply obliged, but I shall receive it in the name of the Lord Jesus Christ.'

"'Oh, well,' said he, 'let us go in the sitting-room and see the women.'

"It so happened that the Mercer Street brethren were disappointed in their movement, and I felt in honor compelled to withdraw any claim I might have on what had occurred before, and for a considerable time after they occupied their church. After that long and tiresome suspense, again the church was offered me. I did not know that the Commodore had not changed his mind. I had not talked with him on the subject since I announced that I was compelled to give up the church. But when the time came I walked in and said : 'Commodore, this church is again in the market, and I can get it if I renew my proposition to them.'

"Said he :

"'Offer them the $50,000 cash. The property is worth it, and always will be worth it, even with the ground-rent. Fix the day for the transfer.'

"Through my friend, the late Gen. James Lorimer Graham, this was done. The Commodore went to Saratoga. I communicated to him the day when the papers were to be made. He directed me to call at his office, which I did, and when I entered his clerk, Mr. Wardell, said : 'Doctor, here is a package containing $50,000 of money from Commodore Vanderbilt for you.'

"I said to him :

"'Do you know what this $50,000 is for?'

"'No, sir, I don't.' ·

"'Didn't the Commodore tell you?'

"'No, sir.'

"'Shall I give you a receipt?'

" ' No, sir.'

" ' Why don't you take a receipt? '

" ' The Commodore didn't tell me to take one.'

"And that is the way I got the Church of the Strangers. I desired to have it put in charge of a body of trustees of prominent gentlemen selected from the principal Churches in New York; but the Commodore refused to do so, saying:

" ' No. You hammer away at some of those fellows about their sins, and they will turn around and be-devil you, so that you will have to quit the church. I am going to give it to you personally.'

" He subsequently made the deeds of settlement so that the pastor should have a life estate in the prop-erty, and that at his death it should fall into the hands of the trustees of the Church of the Strangers appointed according to law. And thus we got the church.

" He lived seven years after that, and never by deed or word or look did he make me feel that he felt that I was under obligation to him. On the contrary, from that day forth he always treated me as one gentleman treats another who has done him a very great favor. It was done in a princely style, and I do believe God paid him and his family a thousand-fold in many ways."

IV.

1870.

New Quarters.

THE events of the last chapter took place during the summer of 1870. The Pastor at once set to work making the necessary repairs. As for several years the congregation which had been occupying the building had been expecting to make some arrangement for removal, the property was neglected, and very much had to be done. $10,000 should have been expended upon it, but the Pastor ventured only half that amount, and supervised all the repairs. He had so little trained his people to work, having had nothing for them to work upon, that he was compelled to do nearly the whole of this alone, while continuing his ministration in the little chapel. Not an officer of the Church visited the premises during the repairs. When all was done, he went to his friend, Commodore Vanderbilt, and told him that the repairs were all finished, and that service would be held on the first Sunday of the next month, October, and that it had cost $5,000 to make the repairs. The Commodore said : " Well, Doctor, how are you going to pay for it?" The reply was; "I do not know, sir,"—for the Doctor thought probably the Commodore would assume the debt. Instead of doing so, he said:

"Neither do I." It afterwards transpired that the Commodore did this to try the Pastor's "pluck," and further to satisfy himself that his confidence in the Doctor's ability was not misplaced. The Pastor arose, saying, "But I will pay it, Commodore,"— and left. He went immediately down into Wall Street, and through a friend, Mr. Charles W. Keep, borrowed the money on his own personal credit, and paid for all the material used and all the work done in repairing the building. This load he bore for some time before he could obtain enough, above what was necessary annually for the running of the Church, to liquidate the debt, but it was finally accomplished.

On Sunday, the 28th of August, the Sunday School had taken possession of its department in the chapel, under the superintendency of Mr. William J. Wood-ward. The building which the "Church of the Strangers" was now to occupy is of historical interest. When that portion of the city was almost in the country, and a number of members of the old Brick Church,* which was then under the pastorate of Dr. Gardiner Spring, separated themselves in order to build a new up-town church, they selected this spot. To that congregation, and to the old St. Mark's Episcopal Church, in the Bowery, almost all the principal families of the city belonged. To the new Presbyterian Church the Rev. Dr. Thomas E. Skinner, as we have seen, was called as its first Pastor.

---

* This Church occupied the block now covered by the "Potter" and "Times" buildings.

The great revival services under the Rev. Dr. Kirk, in 1839-1840, had taken place within those walls. In what is now the Pastor's study, in the chapel facing on Greene Street, were heard the first classes of the Union Theological Seminary, which now has a noble residence at 1200 Park Avenue. All the commencements of the Theological Seminary were held here until 1871. In what is now the parlor of the church there was a Sunday School, in which men and women who have since distinguished themselves in Church work, in literature, and in the department of teaching, received their training.

We are indebted to Mr. R. R. McBurney, Secretary of the Y. M. C. A. in this city, for the following facts:

" On the evening of May 28, 1852, a meeting was held in the lecture-room of what is now the Church of the Strangers, which had been called by a few young men, members of evangelical Churches in this city, who had previously, on several occasions, met together to consider the propriety of forming a Young Men's Christian Association. About three hundred young men assembled at that time, who manifested a deep interest in the object; and it became evident that such an association might be formed with every prospect of usefulness.

"The chair was occupied by Rev. G. T. Bedell, D.D., then Rector of the Church of the Ascension, · Tenth Street and Fifth Avenue, now Protestant Episcopal Bishop of Ohio, who expressed a fervent interest in the cause.

" Rev. C. J. Warren also took part in the exercises; and an admirable address was delivered by the late Rev. Isaac Ferris, D.D., then Pastor of the Market Street Reformed Dutch Church, which embodied a lucid exhibition of the nature and the probable benefits of the proposed organization.

" After the address, the names of one hundred and seventy-three young men were enrolled as members, J. W. Benedict, Esq., acting as chairman.

" At several successive meetings, held in the same place, the proposed Constitution was brought forward, and after being fully discussed, was finally adopted in nearly its present shape.

" On the evening of the 30th of June, 1852, the Association was permanently organized by the election of its officers.

" From the pulpit of the church was delivered the first Annual Sermon before the Young Men's Christian Association, by Rev. Dr. Ferris, who was afterward Chancellor of the University of the City of New York."

THE OPENING.

On Sunday, October 2, 1870, the Church of the Strangers was duly opened. The following account of the opening exercises is taken from the three programmes issued during the days of its continuance:

SUNDAY, OCTOBER 2, 1870.

MORNING, 10.30 o'clock.—Singing the L. M. Doxology, " Praise God, from whom all blessings flow," etc.   *The First Morning Lesson.*—The Hymn, " I love thy kingdom, Lord," 33d of " Hymns for all Christians."   *The Creed.—Prayer.*—By Joseph Holdich, D.D., American Bible Society.   *The Second Morning Lesson.*

HYMN WRITTEN FOR THE OCCASION BY PHŒBE CARY.

Come down, O Lord, and with us live !
    For here with tender, earnest call,
The Gospel Thou didst freely give,
    We freely offer unto all.

Come, with such power and saving grace,
    That we shall cry, with one accord,
" How sweet and awful is this place,
    This sacred temple of the Lord.

Let friend and stranger. one in Thee,
    Feel with such power Thy Spirit move,
That every man's own speech shall be,
    The sweet eternal speech of love.

Yea, fill us with the Holy Ghost,
    Let burning hearts and tongues be given,
Make this a day of Pentecost,
    A foretaste of the bliss of Heaven !

Sermon.—By Robert S. Moran, D.D., Methodist Episcopal Church, South.   *Address.*—By Abel Stevens, D.D., LL.D., Methodist Episcopal Church. At the conclusion of the Morning Service, the Pastor, in his address, among other things, returned thanks for the many attentions the Church had received from its friends, and alluded to the motto in the flowers on the Communion table, " All for Jesus," and said that should now be the motto of the Church of the Strangers.

AFTERNOON, 2.30 o'clock.—Baptism of infants.
3.00 o'clock.—*The Holy Communion*, conducted by
the Pastor, assisted by Thomas H. Skinner, LL.D. ;
George L. Prentiss, D.D., Pastor of the Church of the
Covenant; Robert R. Booth, D.D., Pastor of the
University Place Presbyterian Church (these three
gentlemen having been pastors of the Mercer Street
Church); Gardiner Spring, LL.D.; William B.
Sprague, D.D.; John P. Durbin (one of the Secre-
taries of the Methodist Missionary Society); A. C.
Wedekind, D.D., Pastor of St. James (Lutheran);
Rev. R. Kœnig, of Pesth, Hungary, and other clergy-
men.

EVENING, 7.30 o'clock: *Prayer.*—By Philip Schaff,
D.D., Prof. Union Theological Seminary. *Sermon.—*
By John Cotton Smith, D.D., Rector of the Church
of the Ascension, Protestant Episcopal. *Address.—*
By Mancius C. Hutton, D.D., Pastor Washington
Square Reformed (Dutch) Church.

At the conclusion of the Evening Service Dr.
Deems read the following stanzas, which had been
sent him during the day:

"ALL FOR JESUS."

WRITTEN FOR THE "CHURCH OF THE STRANGERS," BY MRS. M. A. KIDDER.

This holy, peaceful, Sabbath Day,
We bow our inmost hearts and pray
    To Thee, O Jesus!
And while we give afresh to Thee
This Christian Church. so broad, so free,
Our voices and our hearts agree,
    'Tis all for Jesus!

This structure, with its rocky bands,
This holy temple as it stands.
            Was built for Jesus!
The very floor beneath our feet—
The walls that catch the echoes sweet—
This pulpit, aye, and every seat,
            Belong to Jesus.

The Strangers' Church! the world's wide home
Where all, yea all, may freely come,
            And learn of Jesus :
The rich, the poor, the grave and gay,
The lonely wanderers by the way,
May hear God's word, and sing and pray
            To blessed Jesus!

Oh! generous heart, that gave so much;
Oh! open hands, whose gentle touch
            Was seen by Jesus!
Oh! sisters kind and brothers true ;
Oh! loving friends in every pew,
Whate'er we've done, whate'er we do,
            Is all for Jesus!

MONDAY EVENING, OCTOBER 3.

7.30 o'clock, *Public Meeting.*—Rev. Chancellor
Ferris presided. *Vice-Presidents :* Gorham D. Ab-
bott, LL.D., William H. Alexander, Albert T. Bled-
soe, LL.D., Nathan Bishop, LL.D., A. T. Briggs,
Theophilus P. Brouwer, George W. Clarke, Ph.D.,
Charles C. Colgate, Peter Cooper, William C.
Churchill, A.M., Lyman Denison, Daniel Drew, Cor-
nelius R. Disosway,˙ Hon. Wm. E. Dodge, Thomas
C. Doremus, Hon. Wm. M. Evarts, John Elliott,
James Lorimer Graham, Richard C. Gardner, Hon.
Wm. F. Havemeyer, Thomas A. Hoyt, Edward S.

Jaffray, Morris K. Jesup, John H. Keyser, Dr. Jared
Linsly, R. R. Mcburney, Belden Noble, Ex-Gov.
Olden, of N. J., John W. Quincy, John A. Stewart, .
Algernon S. Sullivan, Ex-Gov. Throop, of N. Y.,
John F. Trow, John Elliott Ward, Horace Webster,
LL.D., A. R. Wetmore, Stewart L. Woodford.

Prayer.—By George R. Crooks, D.D., Editor of
The Methodist.

The meeting was a profoundly interesting one.
Dr. Deems gave a history of the rise and progress
of the Church of the Strangers, and of the work
proposed to be accomplished. He was followed by
the Rev. Mr. Kœnig, Pastor of a similar Church in
Pesth, Hungary; and by Hon. Wm. E. Dodge, in a
most happy address of endorsement and congratula-
tion; and by Dr. S. Irenæus Prime, of the New York
Observer, in a most touching and beautiful speech.

TUESDAY, OCTOBER 4.

Rev. Dr. Armitage, of the Fifth Avenue Baptist
Church, preached a most impressive sermon.

FRIDAY EVENING, OCTOBER 7.

7.30 o'clock.—*Public Temperance Meeting,* under
the direction of the Fidelity Temple of Honor. The
Grand Worthy Chief Templar, Calvin E. Keach,
of Rensselaer County, presided. Prayer by Rev.
Stephen Merritt, Jr., Chaplain of Fidelity Temple.
Addresses by Templar William S. Stevenson, Rev. C.
F. Deems, D.D., Hon. B. E. Hale, of Kings County.
Sacred and temperance songs by a young lady.

SUNDAY, OCTOBER 9.

MORNING, 10.20 o'clock: *Prayer.*—By Thomas C. DeWitt, D.D., Collegiate Reformed Church. *Sermon.*—By William E. Munsey, D.D., Methodist Episcopal Church, South. *Address.*—By Rev. George J. Mingins, Superintendent of City Missions.

AFTERNOON, 2.30 o'clock.—Baptism of adults. 3.00 o'clock.—*Sunday School Concert*, conducted by Philip Phillips. The Address by William H. C. Price, Esq., former Superintendent of the School.

EVENING, 7.30 o'clock: *Sermon.*—By Leonard Bacon, D.D., Congregational. *Address.*—By the Pastor.

V.

Internal Economy.

1. MEMBERSHIP.

WHEN any one wishes to join the Church he applies to the Advisory Council. The following is the form of application:

"In applying for membership in the Church of the Strangers, I pledge myself, if accepted, to do what I can to promote the prosperity of the Church in all its departments; to continue a weekly subscription to the support thereof, as the Lord shall prosper me, so long as that is the rule of the Church; and, whenever my address shall be changed, to notify the Pastor promptly."

"Date,...................................... ....

"Name, ...

"Address, ...

"Reference,......................................."

This application is signed by the candidate, in duplicate, and when a favorable action is had one copy is forwarded to the Pastor and the other to the applicant, who is to be present at the ensuing Communion, when he is presented to the Church and by them received into fellowship. If the applicant have a Letter Dismissory from another Church, he refers to that ; otherwise satisfactory reference must be furnished.

Before action is taken the candidate is asked the following questions :

1. Have you truly and earnestly repented of your sins ?

2. Do you believe in our Lord Jesus Christ as your present and sufficient Saviour?

3. Are you in Love and Charity with all men? And especially do you love the society of Christian people ?

4. Will you endeavor, by God's help, to lead a life of holy self-denial and Christian effort for the salvation of others?

5. Have you been baptized?

Baptism is administered according to the mode which satisfies the conscience of the candidate.

The Advisory Council consists of seven members annually nominated by the Pastor and elected by the Monthly Meeting. With the Pastor they determine the admission of candidates. When in their opinion the connection of any one with this Church ceases to promote the cause of Christ, and the Pastor concurs, the connection is dissolved, and the action is announced to the Monthly Meeting, and this is the only announcement required. The Pastor cannot alone dissolve the connection, neither can the Advisory Council : the action must be co-ordinate.

The Monthly Meeting is the authoritative body of the Church. It consists of all the members of the Church.

At its Annual Meeting, at the close of the year, it elects the following officers, viz.: *A President, Vice-President,* and *Clerk* of the Monthly Meeting; *Trustees,* of whom there are nine, three elected annually; an *Advisory Council* of seven; and a *Sunday School Superintendent.* The Advisory Council and the Superintendent of the Sunday School are nominated by the Pastor, as they are his assistants in the spiritual departments of the Church. But the Monthly Meeting may refuse to elect any special nominee; in which case the Pastor must make another nomination. All other offices are filled on open nomination, by a majority of the members present. In the election of Trustees, each contributor to the support of the Church has a vote.

The President of the Monthly Meeting presides at all its sessions, and in his absence the Vice-President. If neither be present, a President, *pro tempore*, is elected by the meeting.

No constitution has ever been framed. As any need arose it was provided for by special actions. These have so shaped the government of the Church, that the above may be taken as a description of its organic structure.

There are a few points in the statement which perhaps need elucidation. Certain officers are nominated by the Pastor, and others are elected without his nomination. The Sunday School Superintendent is one of the former. The superintendent of a Sunday School should be an assistant pastor. The Sunday School should be held in the closest relations to the

Church. The children should be collected therein
with a view to their becoming church members. That
is our theory. Now, it is quite easy to see that if the
office of superintendent were open for promiscuous
nomination and for election by the whole body of
church members, there would frequently be superin-
tendents incompetent for the post, and otherwise ob-
jectionable ; and this might come to pass without any
evil intention on the part of anybody. Out of compliment, a very young man or very young woman, or
some other unfit person, might be nominated for superintendent. After the nomination it might seem
ungracious, it might really give pain, and it might, perhaps, make mischief to the Church, if that person were
not elected. Suppose it were left to the teachers to
appoint a superintendent : that would tend to make
the Sunday School a wholly independent body, and
the Church might be fought by the School. A majority of the teachers might not be members of the
Church. The meetings of the teachers might be used
to breed discontent with the Church.

The Church of the Strangers was an experiment
upon a new line, whòlly unknown to its Pastor. Without any precedent by which to work, the Sunday
School passed through all these difficulties, until the
Pastor had almost begun to believe that a Sunday
School was a curse to the church to which it was in
any wise attached. · It was determined to put the
nomination in the hands of the Pastor. It was a great
responsibility, but one which no pastor should refuse.
Our theory is this : The Pastor is to nominate ; if the

Monthly Meeting do not confirm the nomination he must nominate again ; and so proceed until a Superintendent is elected. The Superintendent is responsible to the Pastor, and has the appointment of each teacher. The teacher holds his, or her, place at the will of the Superintendent. The Superintendent holds his place at the will of the Pastor.

Since that plan was adopted we have had quiet and progress in the Sunday School.

The Church is not a machine. The Pastor thereof is no more a despot than is the father of a family. It is to be presumed that his whole soul is engaged in promoting the happiness and spiritual prosperity of the Church. In selecting a superintendent for nomination, it may be supposed that he would strive to find a man who had the natural endowments, the acquired qualifications, and the spiritual life necessary for this great and delicate work. And then he would strive to find some such man, if possible, as would be agreeable to the teachers. But if he found a man that ought to take the place, though not agreeable to the teachers, the teachers could retire; there is nothing to bind them ; but the Sunday School will go on. It saves cliques, and heart-burnings, and intrigues.

The greatest part of the work is on the Pastor, who makes the selection ; but if, because he does not like to assume that responsibility, he throws it amongst the teachers, or into the Church generally, there will most certainly come upon him difficulties and troubles much greater than those which he will encounter in taking the initial step.

It is also provided that the Advisory Council shall be nominated by the Pastor. The Advisory Council are the seven members of the Church who stand nearest to the Pastor; the men with whom he must have frequent and confidential interviews in regard to matters affecting the most delicate interests of all the members. They must be entirely agreeable to him; one single fractious member would destroy the unity of the body and obstruct the work of the Pastor.

At first sight the statement of the functions of the Advisory Council may seem harsh, and appear to flavor of what people imagine the Star Chamber to have been. A majority of the Advisory Council elects a candidate to membership if the Pastor concur. A majority of the Advisory Council dissolves the connection of the Church and the member, if the Pastor concur. The Pastor cannot of himself enter the name of any person, however saintly, on the roll of membership. The Pastor cannot of himself strike from the roll the name of a convicted felon. Neither can a majority of the Advisory Council do either of these things; but co-ordinately the Pastor and Advisory Council may do both.

Whatever may be the appearance of this arrangement, in the Church of the Strangers it has worked admirably well through a series of years, and, it seems to us, would work well under any Pastor who had the common sense a man ought to have to be in charge of a Church. It is not to be supposed, in the first place, that a Pastor would nominate seven men for an Advisory Council, and that the whole Church would confirm that nomination, if those men were not persons of sufficient character, judgment, and piety to be entrusted with such a function. It is not to be supposed that seven men so elected and advertised to the world, and responsible both to the Church of the Strangers and to public opinion, would find a majority of their members willing to do an unjust and unchristian thing toward any brother, even the humblest member of the Church. It is not to be supposed that a pastor responsible to a Church of over six hundred communicants and to the public would confirm an act of ecclesiastical tyranny.

Congregational and Independent Churches have been split by referring such cases to the whole body of the Church. It is possible for the worst man in any town to enter a Church as a member. We know that there is no man brought to trial before a body of men, women, and children, numbering several hundreds, who could not get up a small, or large, party to stand by him. This curse of Church trials has been a widespread affliction. We determined to have no Church trials in the Church of the Strangers.

If any brother is walking in such a way as does not seem to promote the cause of Christ, the Pastor or the Advisory Council, or some member of the latter, will endeavor to bring him to a sense of his duty; will labor with him; will do all that their judgment suggests to continue him in the Church a reformed and saved man.

No Church can wish to lose members, and no Church that has the spirit of the Master will fail to do every-

thing to retain a member so long as there is any hope
that he will discontinue such a course of life as is in-
jurious to Christianity.

Several such cases have occurred in our history, and
very few cases have been such as to compel the Advisory Council and the Pastor to dissolve a member's
connection with the Church for cause. As an illustration : A member of the Church took to drink. It
was an old inherited proclivity of his, which he was
supposed to have learned to conquer before he became a member of the Church. When it broke upon
him afresh his brethren talked and prayed with him.
He came before the Advisory Council and said to
them : " Brethren, my case is this : If I take a glass of
wine, my self-control is gone and I must go through
my spree. I will endeavor to avoid the occasion
hereafter. I am exceedingly sorry this has occurred ;
I pray God it may not occur again, and I ask your
prayers. Now, brethren, if the Church drop me I am
afraid I am lost, although, even outside, I shall attend
the Church, and fight the devil. Brethren, if you
think the Church of the Strangers is going to be
injured by my continuance in it, you must do your
duty and drop me ; but if you can see your way clear,
on my penitence, and confession and promise, to keep
me, I shall be forever grateful for your brotherly kindness and forbearance."

He was a cultivated man, a man in a large business
down-town. Now, what was a Church to do in a case
of that kind ? We did not dismiss him. Similar cases
have occurred with men who had little education and

no position, and we have pursued the same course.
In several cases they were saved. The gentlemen
alluded to above, and other men in similar cases, have
died in the Church. So successful has this proved in
doing good to souls and in saving the Church from
quarrels, tumults, and disruptions, that we confidently
commend it to the serious consideration of the
Churches as a most valuable measure.

In regard to the relation between the Church and
the member we hold this theory: Any member con-
siders it his right at any moment to leave the Church
with or without notice, and, even when notice is given,
with or without assigning a reason. In a free country
like ours perhaps this is true. The question arises
whether, on the other hand, the Church has not the
same right to retire from its connection with the member. Who shall say that it has not? Has a member
a right to demand a letter? We think not, any more
than one gentleman has a right to demand a letter of
introduction from one who has been his friend to that
friend's friend. It is with the giver of the letter to
say whether it shall be given or not. No man has a
right to demand it. Where a member has been in
good standing and announces his desire of becoming
a member of another Church, it seems to be the duty
of the Church which he leaves promptly to tender a
kind and cordial letter of commendation to the Church
which he wishes to join. We think that no pastor with
a true sense of Christian propriety would for one moment strive to keep in his Church any member who sig-
nified the slightest desire of moving to another Church.

Nor would he hesitate to do all in his power to make the transfer agreeable to the member leaving, to the Church he has left, and to the Church which is to acquire his membership. That seems to us to be the right relation of the parties. At any rate, on that we have acted, and have found it to work well.

SUMMARY OF MEMBERSHIP.

Date.	Confession.	Letter.	Total.	Dismissions.	Net Increase.	Total at close of Year.
1868	13	49	62	5	57	57
1869	19	31	50	5	45	102
1870	18	47	65	15	50	152
1871	37	70	107	17	90	242
1872	63	61	124	24	100	342
1873	35	42	77	17	60	402
1874	54	44	98	36	62	463
1875	16	30	46	47	Dec.	462
1876	85	48	133	88	45	507
1877	47	32	79	43	36	544
1878	45	31	76	60	16	560
1879	51	35	86	58	28	588
1880	27	21	48	110	Dec., 62*	526
1881	46	38	84	46	38	564
1882	36	25	61	48	13	577
1883	39	50	89	69	22	599
1884	42	30	72	68	4	603
1885	34	41	75	73	2	605
1886	33	30	63	52	11	616

There have been received into the Church during the first nineteen years 1,497 persons—740 on confession of faith, and 757 by letter. There have been

* The Pastor was absent six months in 1880, and upon his return the books were revised, and all names erased except those of actual members.

taken from the roll by removals. deaths, etc.. 881.
Total on the roll at the close of 1886. 616.

The location of the building and the composition
of the congregation are such as to render frequent removals on the part of members inevitable. Those by
letter have come from Baptist, Church of England,
Congregational. Dutch Reformed. Free Church of
Scotland. Independent, Lutheran. Methodist-Episco-
pal (North and South). Presbyterian. Protestant-Epis-
copal, Mennonite. and Wesleyan Churches. In their
nationalities the members represent twenty-nine
States of the Union. and Canada. New Brunswick,
Nova Scotia. England. Scotland. Ireland. Wales,
France. Spain. Holland. Italy, Germany. Sweden,
Switzerland. Denmark. Turkey, China, South Amer-
ica. Cuba. Bermuda, and Prince Edward's Isle.

2. THE BOARD OF FINANCE.

The Board of Finance is constituted as follows: At
their Annual Meeting. the Board of Trustees elect one
of their members to be Treasurer of the Church and
another to be Financial Secretary of the same. These
two officers and the President of the Board of Trustees, together with two other members of that body
elected at the same time. are the Board of Finance
and Executive Committee of the Church. having
charge of all the financial matters. The President of
the Board of Trustees is also President *ex officio* of
the Board of Finance. In other words. the Board of
Finance is a Committee of Trustees appointed by the

Trustees and charged with the financial and executive functions of the Church.

The Treasurer receives all the Sunday collections, all donations and special collections, and, at the end of each month from the Financial Secretary all the money received by the latter from subscribers during the month. He makes all payments on account of the Church upon the approval of the Board of Finance, and makes monthly, quarterly, and annual reports of all receipts and disbursements. His annual report is printed and distributed among the members of the Church.

The Financial Secretary keeps a record of the proceedings of the Board of Finance ; also the accounts of the subscribers to the support of the Church. He receives all subscription moneys, and at the end of each month turns them over to the Treasurer. His quarterly report is printed for distribution, and contains acknowledgments for all sums received.

3. SUPPORT OF THE CHURCH.

To maintain the Church, the disbursements are for the Pastor, Sunday School, music, sexton, repairs, printing, cleaning, heating, lighting, insurance, and clerical help.

The Church receives *no income from pew rents. All the seats are free. It has no endowment.* The income is derived from three sources: 1. Collections at Sunday services ; 2. Donations ; 3. Subscriptions. Every *member* of the Church is *pledged* to make a weekly subscription of some stated amount; but the whole amount for the month, the quarter, or the year may be paid at one time, if preferred. Every *regular attendant* is *expected* to become a subscriber of a stated amount.

The following is the form of subscription now (1887) in use, and may be obtained from the Financial Secretary:

FORM OF SUBSCRIPTION.

The Church of the Strangers depends for financial support upon the voluntary donations and the subscriptions of its friends and members.

I promise to pay to the Treasurer of the CHURCH OF THE STRANGERS, the amount stated below until I otherwise direct; also to notify promptly the Financial Secretary of any change in my address.

Name..

P. O. Address.................................

Weekly Subscriptions, $........   ....Cts.

Date, 1st of..............188

When filled, return to ...., ..., New York.

It is believed that there are none too poor to subscribe some amount. For system, it is desired that those who wish to contribute largely should conform to the same rules that govern smaller subscribers. If one wishes to give $50 a year, his subscription should read, "$1.00 a week": if $500 a year, "$10.00 a week."

The subscription blanks are kept on file by the

Financial Secretary. Upon the receipt of a blank, he assigns a *number to the subscriber*, who is also furnished with a supply of small envelopes, to be used weekly. In all reports of money received the number is used, and not the name of the subscriber.

The Financial Secretary keeps a book containing a list of subscribers, with their numbers opposite each name. In another part of the book each *number* has a space allotted to it, with fifty-two ruled columns, representing the weeks of a year.

Subscribers are requested, in making payments, to see that the amount covers a certain number of weeks, and not parts of weeks. These weekly subscriptions are dropped into boxes at the doors, marked, "For the Church." The Financial Secretary collects these envelopes, counts the money to see that the amount in each agrees with the memorandum on the outside, and credits the subscriber for as many weeks as the money covers. None save the Board of Finance are ever permitted to inspect the accounts of subscribers.

The Pastor himself is not to know whether any member of the Church is a subscriber or not. No member of the Church is to talk to him about his subscription. It is deemed best that he should not have anything to do with the financial support of the Church, so that he may give his whole life to its spiritual upbuilding. Being questioned to-day (March 11, 1887), he said : "No, I do not know whether a single member of the Board of Trustees, or of the Advisory Council, or whether the Superintendent of

the Sunday School, or any teacher, is a subscriber to
our sustentation fund. The only member whom
I know to be a subscriber is my wife, and one or two
others who incidentally have spoken to me of their
subscription. I like this plan. When I am talking
to a member of the Church, I do not know whether
he gives one cent a year or ten dollars a week to
carry forward the Church, so I am wholly unaffected
in my intercourse with my people by considerations
of that sort."

It will be seen that in a Church of over six hundred
members such a system as this will be very laborious,
but we have found ordinarily the most competent
men willing, for the sake of the Church, to perform
the work. Very seldom has the congregation had
appeals to bring up the finances. Several wealthy
families have been lost to the Church, families willing
to pay large amounts for separate pews, but not
willing to run the risk of sitting side by side with
everybody. We have not seen how it was possible
that a Church of the " Strangers " could be managed
in that way; and so we have submitted to these dis-
abilities in order to carry out the design of the
Church.

We believe the members of our congregation are as
well content with this plan as they could be with any
other, and there are hundreds of worshipers who feel
free and comfortable in our Church who, with all
their intelligence and piety, could not be made comfortable in a Church that had rented pews. As it is
found that persons like particular places, our ushers

are careful not to put others in those places; and there are always seats just as good elsewhere in the Church.

4. THE USHERS.

Among our standing committees is one called the Committee of Hospitality, whose duty it is to meet strangers at the door and show them to seats, and otherwise make them comfortable. They are not to discriminate between strangers and regular attendants as against the former. They are carefully taught not to fall into the error set forth by St. James: "My brethren, have not the faith of our Lord Jesus Christ, the Lord of glory, with respect of persons. For if there come unto your assembly a man with a gold ring, in goodly apparel, and there come in also a poor man in vile raiment; and ye have respect to him that weareth the gay clothing, and say unto him, Sit thou here in a good place; and say to the poor, Stand thou there, or sit here under my footstool: are ye not then partial in yourselves, and are become judges of evil thoughts? Hearken, my beloved brethren, Hath not God chosen the poor of this world rich in faith, and heirs of the kingdom which he hath promised to them that love him?"

As much attention is paid to him that comes with a patch on his clothes, as to him that comes with a diamond blazing on his bosom. This Church belongs as much to the strangers from other cities and from country places as it does to those who are communicants of our regular Church organization; indeed, if there be any difference, the strangers have the very first claim. The intent is that they shall have a church in which—of whatever denomination they may be at their residences—they shall feel at home when they come to worship God with us. We believe that strangers appreciate this and remember it in the regular *offertory* of the Church, and in occasional special donations, and in legacies. Dr. Deems tells the following story:

Once a gentleman came into my study, and said: "I have never spoken to you, Doctor, but I have been a very regular attendant on the Church services. This spring I had business in Texas, and this business carried me up to that border of the State which is near New Mexico. I did not feel that it was altogether safe traveling. One day I met three men who were armed *cap-a-pie.* They halted me, and questioned me uncomfortably closely as to my incomings and outgoings. One of them eyed me sharply through the colloquy which I had with his comrade. At last he said, ' Stranger, I'm on the trail of ye. Ain't you from the Church of the Strangers?' I was much surprised at the question, and replied that when in New York my custom was to worship on Sunday mornings at the Church of the Strangers. 'Have *you* ever been there?' I asked. Said he, 'I'll tell you how it was. Me and Bill were drivin' our cattle, and sold 'em for a big chunk. Ses Bill to me, " Look here, Jim ; let's go on a lark to New York," and I agreed. We got thar Saturday, and saw in the papers notice of a good many meetin's on Sunday, and Bill saw thar was a

Church of the Strangers, and where it was, and ses
to me, "Look here, Jim; we don't often have a chance
at home; I reckon we oughter go to meetin', and
here's the Church of the Strangers." So down we
steered thar, and when we got to the door we were a
little shy. We had lost our meetin' habits, and didn't
know how to behave. A dapper little feller steps up
to us, and ses, "Gentlemen, mayn't I show you
seats?" We told him that was what we come for,
and, sure 'nough, if we had been that chap's first
cousin, he could not have been smilin'er nor kinder
than he was. He just marched Bill and me up to
the deacon's pew and right in front of old Commodore Vanderbilt's pew, and I tell ye we had to behave! How are them fellows anyway—the boys that
meet strangers at the door? Give 'em my love. I
just think they're prime.' His comrade joined in this
eulogy of the ushers. I talked with them a great
deal about you, and we got to be fast friends, and
those men loaded me with every kindness until we
parted. I did not know how to communicate this to
your ushers, so I tell it to you." Of course the
Pastor was delighted to tell this story, which he has
frequently done since to the Committee on Hospitality.

It is believed that this feature of church politeness
was first begun in this city in the Church of the
Strangers; it has become so common that now
almost all the churches are given to hospitality. But
history records the beginnings of things which are now
so general as no longer to be regarded as singular.

5. OUR SYMBOL OF FAITH.

As the Church of the Strangers is an independent Christian Church, it could not adopt any articles of religion or Confession of Faith which distinctly marks any of the different sects in church or schools in theology. It was deemed advisable, therefore, to adopt the Apostles' Creed as a symbol commended by its antiquity, and by the fact that it is believed that it can be repeated from the heart by Christian people of all denominations. The form in which it is used in the Church of the Strangers has two modifications:

(*a*) Where it is said of Christ, that " He descended into Hell," we repeat, " He went to the place of departed spirits," an alternative form also sometimes used in other churches.

(*b*) In the conclusion of the Creed, after "I believe in the Holy Ghost," come the words, " Holy Catholic Church, the communion of Saints." Because uninstructed persons may confound ideas in the employment of the words, " Holy Catholic Church," we use the phrase, " Holy Church of God, the communion of Saints," punctuating with a comma instead of a semicolon after the word " God," so that that part of our Creed sets forth our belief that there is "a Holy Church of God," and that church is the " communion of Saints;" and that all who are striving to be good are in the " Holy Church of God."

6. OUR RITUAL.

The Ritual of the Church is very simple. At the Morning Service, when the Pastor enters the pulpit,

he repeats some passage of Scripture, ordinarily this :
"The Lord is in His holy temple; let all the earth
keep silence before Him." The congregation then
engage in silent prayer, after which a voluntary is sung
by the choir. Then the Pastor reads the Epistle and
the Gospel for the day, as appointed in the Book
of Common Prayer, frequently commenting upon it.
After these lessons a hymn is sung, at the conclusion
of which the whole congregation unite in repeating the
Apostles' Creed. After the Creed the Pastor makes a
call to prayer and leads the whole congregation in
their devotions, all joining in the Lord's Prayer at
the conclusion. After this prayer notices are given of
Church work during the week; then follows the second lesson, generally selected in reference to the subject of the discourse; a hymn is sung; the sermon is
delivered, which is followed by a prayer. After prayer,
while the children of the " Half-Orphan Asylum " sing
a hymn, the collection is taken up. Services are
closed by the singing of the "Gloria" or long metre
doxology beginning, "Praise God, from whom all
blessings flow;" and finally the Apostolic benediction, pronounced by the Pastor.

At the Evening Service the Creed and the appointed
lessons are omitted. The rest of the order is followed,
the Pastor ordinarily selecting one lesson from the
Old Testament, and one lesson from the New Testament.

The orphan children are not present in the evening.
These children belong to the Half-Orphan Asylum on
Tenth Street, near Sixth Avenue. About two hun-

dred of them attend the Morning Service in the Church
of the Strangers, and have their places in the gallery
near the choir. Five generations of these children
have passed through the Church during the last twenty
years. Some of them have become communicants of
the Church of the Strangers, some of other churches,
and many of them have grown up to be excellent men
and women, and have engaged in Christian work. One
of the girls for two years has taken waifs from the city
into a country place, to give them a little summer vacation from the heat of the city. She is now married.
The songs of these little children through all these
years have been a great blessing. The Pastor says
that he has frequently heard men very much hardened
by worldly business, in distant parts of the country,
who have spoken, sometimes with tears in their eyes,
of the manner in which they were touched by the songs
sung by the little ones in the gallery.

7. THE HOLY COMMUNION.

The Holy Communion is administered in the Church
on the first Sunday in every month. For the
last twenty years very seldom has this blessed service
been omitted, and never except when the church was
undergoing repairs. On Communion Sunday the
only change made in the service is the introduction
of the Ten Commandments.

Just before the Creed the Pastor repeats each Com-
mandment, and the people respond, " Lord, have
mercy upon us, and incline our hearts to keep this Thy
law."

After the regular service the Holy Communion is administered. Around the font in front of the pulpit a table is set to accommodate the Pastor and Advisory Council, making eight persons.

The Ritual of the Communion is very much like that of the Protestant Episcopal and Methodist Episcopal Churches. Candidates who have been accepted by the Advisory Council are received into full membership. And a collection for the poor is always taken up.

The communicants are in alternate pews, and, as they come from different denominations of Christians, they can take the Communion in any posture which they consider reverent and profitable. To some the pew in front serves as the railing of the chancel does in Episcopal Churches. Others sit, and others stand, at the moment of taking the bread and wine. There is no insistence upon the details of the Ritual. We believe that all things should be done "decently" and "in order," but that some verge and scope should be allowed to differences of opinion as to what really is the apostolic meaning of these words.

8. BAPTISM.

On the third Sunday in each month Baptism is administered to infants, and on the fourth Sunday to adults. The font is for children, and for those who prefer it to being baptized by immersion. Just under the pulpit is a baptistry for those who prefer immersion. The theory is that the mode is a matter which concerns the candidate, that he must do what will

keep him in good conscience, and that the Pastor is
simply to serve him for Christ's sake in the adminis-
tration of Baptism, "In the name of the Father,
and of the Son, and of the Holy Ghost."

9. OTHER SERVICES.

The Sunday School of the Church is held every
Sunday morning at nine o'clock, in the chapel. The
church on Mercer Street is a stone building; the
chapel, which faces on Greene Street, is a two-story
brick building, and the two structures are entirely
separate. The lower story of the chapel is fitted up
as a parlor.

The Sunday School has a Bible Class for young
men, a Bible Class for young women, a Visitor's
Class; so that those who drop in may have something
to do, and an Infant Class.

At half-past 2 o'clock is the Chinese Sunday
School in the chapel, ordinarily closing at 4 o'clock.

At 6.45 a Vesper service is held in the church
parlor, one of the rooms in the chapel. This is
conducted by our young men, and is a service of
prayer preparatory to the public service in the church.

The regular Prayer Meeting of the Church is on
Friday night, in the church parlor.

A "Mothers' Meeting" is held every Wednesday
following the first Sunday in the month, and on the
second Wednesday thereafter, at 3 o'clock P.M.

There is a Church Sociable every Wednesday evening following the first Sunday.

VI

The Tribes.

THE Holy Communion was administered to the Church of the Strangers on the first Sunday of January, 1868, at the formation of the Church. There has been but one Communion Sunday on which there was no addition to the Church.

A lady whose son was in the far West became so concerned about him that she called upon the Pastor and asked him to observe daily prayer for her distant boy at a certain hour, in which she would join in supplications in her closet. A few weeks after this daily united prayer had begun the son appeared in New York, and reported himself to his mother as having been strangely moved to leave California and return to the city. He accompanied his mother to our service, and the Word of God took such effect upon him that he became a converted man, joined the Church October 2, 1881, and has been walking uprightly in the faith ever since. Just before the October Communion, 1882, he was visiting the Pastor in company with another young man. He said: "Dear Pastor, next Sunday will be the anniversary of the beginning of my Church membership. I feel very grateful to God for having sustained me through the year and enabled me to resist temptation and to 'fight the good fight of faith.' I should like very much if those who joined with me at that time could meet on Monday night and assist me in returning thanks to God." The other young man was so struck with the proposition that he said, inasmuch as he had joined in January, he wished the Pastor would keep it in remembrance also, and so arrange that all those who had joined with *him* should meet on the succeeding Monday night to return thanks to God for His helping grace. Meditating upon this a few minutes, Dr. Deems replied that he did not see why he should not invite all who had joined in any October since the Church began, to assemble together in a sort of *classis*, or band, for the purpose of returning thanks. Nor did he see why all those who had joined at any January Communion should not come together in a friendly devotional meeting. Immediately upon this, one of the three gentlemen, it is not now remembered which, suggested that, as that would bring two sections of the Church together, it might be extended so as to cover the whole Church and have twelve bands. The word twelve struck somebody's ear as a reminder of the Twelve Tribes of Israel, and so, with some leaning to facetiousness, that name was adopted for these several bands of believers. The idea was promptly carried into practical effect.

These Tribes are voluntary combinations. No member is compelled to attend any of the Tribe meetings. Each Tribe elects a patriarch and a scribe, and these two persons have the general oversight of the membership—notification of meetings, visitation of the sick, and such pastoral care, as laymen may take of one another. The scribe is not always a man. It has been found that in some of the Tribes there are ladies with time and skill for the work who are willing to assume it.

This Tribal arrangement has been in many particulars exceedingly useful in providing more thorough spiritual oversight of the whole Church than any one Pastor could give. Each Tribe has an anniversary in the chapel, an annual meeting at the pastor's, and two or three other meetings, usually at private houses, no "refreshments" beyond cold water being allowed. The Tribe manages its own affairs, and the meetings are more or less social, more or less religious, very much according to the temperament of the officers and the members. It affords the pastor additional opportunities of seeing his members and of becoming acquainted with them under social conditions.

PASTORAL VISITING.

From time immemorial this has been one of the perplexing questions in every Church in every large city. The members of the Church of the Strangers reside in different parts of New York City, Brooklyn, and Jersey City. There are some members within the limits of those cities that live twelve miles apart. At this writing there are more members of the Church living between 119th and 134th streets than belonged to it at the time of its organization. It is easily perceived how much time must be consumed in a regular visitation of all these persons. Moreover, in this Church, composed almost entirely of people engaged in business, it is nearly impracticable to maintain regular pastoral visiting. If the Pastor go from house to house he will hardly ever see the men of the family until about six o'clock in the evening, when men ordinarily return to their homes to dinner. In the Church of the Strangers many of the women are engaged in business as artists, clerks, literary helpers, and saleswomen in stores. The women who are at the heads of families are frequently absent from home or entertaining company. The result is that, as the Pastor makes his regular rounds, he misses a majority of his parishioners, and in a large proportion of other cases feels that his call was most inopportune. But there is no Pastor who does not long to know his people. He cannot endure to lose sight of them week after week, until their features fade out of his memory. Some he sees every week in the Church, in the Sunday School, at the Prayer Meetings, and at meetings of the Sisters of the Stranger. But when all these are counted, they make a small minority of the entire Church membership.

For a long time much prayerful study was given to the matter, and as a result the authorities devised a method of meeting the difficulty which, while not perfectly successful, has been helpful and at least removed all cause of complaint.

There is given to every member on the first of the year a membership card, of which the following is a copy:

No. on the Pastor's Record : { This card is to be returned to the Pastor, after the December communion and before Christmas. Be prompt, so that he may make his visiting plans for next year.

𝔍oined the 𝔠hurch of the 𝔖trangers.

This Card becomes void on 31st December, 188......

On the obverse of the card is the following :

COMMUNION RECORD.

[Please place opposite each month *"yes,"* if you were at that month's communion. After your address has been taken this card will be returned to you, as it may be interesting in after years.]

January...
February..
March..
April...
May...
June..
July..
August ....
September ....
October...
November ....
December ....
Has your Pastor visited you this year?...............
Have you visited your Pastor this year?..............
When you return this card write your residence below.

....

This card explains itself. It is the duty of the member to preserve it and hand it in after the December Communion, and before the First of January, with the blanks filled up. The address of each person, as given by himself, is then examined, and the Church-roll corrected thereby. On the First of January we are supposed to know the residence of every communicant. Then a list is made out of those whom the Pastor has not visited during the year, and another list of those who have not visited the Pastor. He has up to this time endeavored each year to visit those upon whom he did not call the year before, so as to be able to make the circuit of the Church entire in, at the farthest, two years.

But what is the object of pastoral visiting? Is it simply to gratify parishioners? Is it simply to satisfy the whole body of parishioners that the Pastor is impartial? These are motives which do not justify the outlay of time and strength. They are very small motives, and the work is very great. It seems to us that the real objects of pastoral visiting are that the Pastor may know the spiritual condition of his congregation, so as to enable him to minister to them from the pulpit more directly and more profitably, and also that he may edify them when he sees them in their houses. A pastoral visit is something different from a social or a business visit. It involves the cure of souls. In New York that can hardly be attained by the Pastor calling upon the members.

In the Church of the Strangers this plan has been fallen upon ; once a week the Pastor gives a whole afternoon and evening to receiving people. And he announces the reception on the preceding Sunday from the pulpit. It is not the same day every week, for the reason that that would exclude some who have particular engagements on certain days or evenings; and the intention is to afford everybody an opportunity to come. It is not a levee; for the Pastor receives each one separately, if necessary, or each family where a whole family come together. There may be twenty or thirty assembled in the front parlor, and they may converse with one another, and thus form Church acquaintances. A few minutes is given to each parishioner or to each group. Sometimes there are few at one of these pastoral receptions and so some interviews are long. Sometimes the Pastor offers more than twenty separate prayers in the afternoon and evening of a reception. The Pastor must judge as to the time, as a physician does at clinic or in office. It has almost always occurred that each one has had sufficient time for the interview. When the hour arrives for closing, if there are two or three in the front parlor, the Pastor ordinarily sees them all together, leads in devotional exercises, and appoints a time to meet each one. Frequently he announces from the pulpit that these hours are not set for the purpose of restricting his people to calling in those hours, but that they may be sure that he will make arrangements to meet them then, adding that, as the Pastor belongs to the Church, any member has a right to call upon him and send for him any hour of the day or night. Those who are sick and need the

Pastor are enjoined to let him know, and then he visits them as promptly as possible. The good of this plan is: that the parishioner leaves his home and avoids all interruptions that could possibly come to him, and he goes to see his Pastor when he knows that his Pastor has laid aside every other study and every other work to devote the time to him.

This arrangement does not make it any easier whatever for the Pastor. It simply enables him to do very much more than could possibly be done in the ordinary loose and irregular way. It is to be remembered that the Church of the Strangers differs from other Churches in the city in this, that the Pastor holds himself bound to visit sick strangers or other strangers that call for his pastoral help.

VII.

The Sunday School.

THE Sunday School of the Church of the Strangers was organized in May, 1867, in the small chapel of the University, while yet the place was known as *The Strangers' Sunday Home.* There were only ten or twelve scholars at first, and Mr. R. C. Daniel was put in charge of them as Superintendent. The next year the Church of the Strangers was organized, and the Sunday School was reorganized, Mr. Daniel resigning, October 11, 1868, and Mr. William H. C. Price being elected to fill the vacancy.

Mr. Price, to the great regret of the entire school, tendered his resignation October 14, 1869, in consequence of his removal to Brooklyn ; and at the solicitation of the Pastor and teachers Mr. Robert H. Johnson accepted the Superintendency temporarily, filling the position until January 1, 1870, when Mr. Otto F. Von Rhein was elected. He resigned May 1, 1870, and Mr. Wm. J. Woodward was chosen, and filled the position until January 1, 1872, when Mr. R. L. Crawford was elected, and served until July following. He resigned, when Mr. W. J. Woodward was again elected to the position, and served until May, 1873, when Mr. Wm. H. C. Price was re-elected, and served until January,

1875. After this Mr. J. H. Schenck served for two months as Superintendent *pro tem.*, and was succeeded by Mr. B. A. Brooks, who served until July, 1879, when Prof. George W. Pettit was elected. He resigned in September, 1886, and Mr. B. Van Henneck, who still retains the office (1887), succeeded.

The School has always had faithful superintendence. Perhaps an unexampled record of punctual and devoted service is that of Prof. Pettit, who, during his seven years of superintendency, though he lived about three miles from school, *was never once absent or late!* It may be added that he always found the Pastor present at the opening.

The School commenced, as we have seen, with ten or twelve scholars. During the first three years the records were imperfectly kept. Below we present a table showing the attendance by years from 1871 to date.

Although this record does not show a vast School, so many former members are scattered over the world that it will be of interest to them to have a record of the progress of the School, while those who are studying the movements of an independent Church, wish to know every particular, and therefore have a right to see the nakedness as well as the wealth of the land.

Moreover, as we have already seen, the members of this Church are so widely scattered that many of their children are unable to attend their own School. It is believed that what is lacking in quantity is largely made up in quality.

REGULAR ATTENDANCE BY YEARS FROM 1871 TO 1887.

Month.	Year.	Superintendents.	Teachers and Officers.	Scholars.	Total.
Jan. 1	1871	Wm. J. Woodward.....	24	126	150
"	1872	R. L. Crawford, W. J. Woodward ..	27	177	204
"	1873	W. J. Woodward, W. H. C. Price. ..	31	278	209
"	1874	W. H. C. Price........	31	243	274
"	1875	J. H. Schenck, B. A. Brooks.	32	269	301
"	1876	B. A. Brooks	23	260	283
"	1877	"	25	189	214
"	1878	"	33.	261	294
"	1879	B. A. Brooks, G. W. Pettit.	33	234	267
"	1880	G. W. Pettit...........	35	203	238
"	1881	"	36	193	229
"	1882	"	36	209	245
"	1883	"	37	156	193
"	1884	"	37	159	196
"	1885	"	37	172	209
"	1886	"	36	226	262

Owing to the great distances at which the families live from the Church, the School was never very large, but every scholar was known and had to be in regular attendance to keep his name upon the roll. The figures given represent the number regularly present, and not the names upon the books.

The sessions of the School begin promptly at 9 A. M. with the singing of a hymn, after which the Pastor of the Church asks the scholars to repeat in concert the Golden Text and Central Truth for the day. The Apostles' Creed is then repeated, followed by prayer by the Pastor, the School joining him at the close in the Lord's Prayer. The Pastor next delivers a short address on some topic suggested by the lesson, or by an incident during the week. These sermonettes are very delightful and helpful to teacher and scholar. They are full of that zeal and hopefulness so characteristic of Dr. Deems, which kindle every heart with renewing energy. The Pastor is as punctually and regularly at the School as if he himself were Superintendent. Nothing but sickness or absence from the city is allowed to come between him and his Sunday School, and he has never been sick except one Sunday.

Singing and reading of the lesson follow the address, after which the class recitations begin. At 10:10 a bell is tapped, which notifies the teachers that within five minutes the lessons are to close. At 10:15 the session closes with a hymn. This gives all time enough to be in Church at 10:30.

Among the features of the School worthy of special mention are the following:

1. *Good Order.*—The discipline of the day schools is stricter than here, but it does not result in better order. The commander-in-chief of these forces is Love, and the obedience rendered is cheerful, not mechanical. The Superintendent never scolds, and rarely speaks to command. One tap of the bell is enough to secure perfect silence. We have seen Sunday Schools where the Superintendent was well nigh distracted by vain efforts to keep order, and where it was no uncommon occurrence to see a refractory youngster publicly disciplined.

In our School order is born of—

2. *The spirit of reverence*, which is the only kind of order *that keeps itself*. It has been said that that is the best government which teaches its subjects to govern themselves. Any kind of authority is bad that fails to inspire respect. In this School there is a very marked spirit of reverence. The boisterous element is entirely subdued, and all is done and said in a manner befitting the house of God. By reverence we do not mean solemnity, lack of spirit, repression ; but a cheerful, healthy tone of spirituality. These two elements naturally result in—

3. *Careful Attention.*—The Superintendent of the public schools in this city will not license any person as a teacher for more than six months in the beginning. This gives the individual a chance to get a trial in the schools. If at the end of six months the person proves himself a poor disciplinarian, his license will not be renewed, no matter how excellent a scholar he may be. Order must be had before instruction can begin.

Conversely, where order is good instruction is easy ; the attention is readily secured and riveted. In this School everybody is busy, teachers and scholars alike intent upon the lesson.

The average age of the pupils is far above the average of Sunday Schools. Very few ever become " too old to go to Sunday School." There are classes for all ages. One class is for " Young Women," another for " Young Men," and a third for " Visitors."

The officers of the School are the Superintendent, the Treasurer, the Secretary and Assistant, and the Librarian and Assistant.

There is a library of about five hundred volumes, which has recently been thoroughly overhauled and supplied with many new books and a new catalogue. At every Monthly Meeting of the Church the Superintendent reads a report setting forth the condition of the School. This meeting appoints a monthly "Visitor," whose duty it is to visit the School and report what might be termed an *outside view* of the same. Through these several channels constant communication is maintained between the School and the Church. At least two of the regular Prayer Meetings of the Church every year are devoted to " Prayer for children and the Sunday School."

THE CHRISTMAS FESTIVAL.

Up to and including the year 1884 the Church of the Strangers followed the general custom of distributing gifts in the form of candies, fruits, toys, books, etc. A committee was appointed to provide the presents, and evergreens for decorative purposes.

Another committee was appointed to provide prize gifts, which were distributed for regular and punctual attendance. All the teachers constituted a general committee to decorate the trees and the school-room. When the time came for the meeting there was always a great crowd. Every child expected something. There was a brilliantly lighted, tastefully decorated room, containing trees loaded with gifts. The exercises consisted ordinarily of an address by the Pastor, singing and recitation by the scholars, one **or two** presentation speeches, the grand distribution of presents, and then the end.

It was an occasion of general interest and rejoicing. The children were as happy as children ever are under similar circumstances. It inculcated in the infant mind a lively sense of the blessedness of *receiving*. It offered a never-failing promise of reward for every child at the close of the year; and it never disappointed a single hope thus begotten. Probably (no proof exists, so far as we know) it kept up the attendance of the School. At any rate it always left upon the pupil's mind the impression that the essence of Christmas joy and of Christianity in general, consisted in *receiving* something. It was a sort of kindergarten to develop the idea of passive church membership. The School was an efficient body of *recipients*. The School was the coach, the teachers were the draught horses, the Superintendent was the driver, and everybody else was having a ride!

Dr. Deems had frequently hinted in his addresses before the School that such festivals as these were unChristian. In 1885 the officers and teachers became convinced that their Pastor was right, and they determined to make a new departure. It was a bold step they now decided on; but the success of the departure proved that the pastoral instruction mentioned above had not fallen upon barren soil. The School was ripe for revolution.

There was to be no longer a candy committee, no expensive decorations, no trees, no presents for the scholars.

The School provided a sufficient number of paper bags to be distributed to the scholars and the members of the Church and congregation on the Sunday preceding Christmas. These were to be filled with dry groceries, toys, books, anything suitable as a present to a poor child or family. The festival was held in the body of the church, and every man, woman, and child who attended it had a paper bag or other parcel, which was delivered to the proper officers detailed to receive such contributions. An immense stock of goods was the result.

A large audience was waiting when the Superintendent rapped for order. There was a hymn, a prayer, followed by the Pastor's address. He called attention to the difference between "hugeness" and "greatness" as applied to a Sunday School. "As this can never be a huge School," he said, "it must endeavor to be a great one." He then asked all the children who had received presents at home to raise hands. Apparently every hand went up. But to be quite certain he demanded if a single child were in the audience that had had no present. No response. "Then," he continued, "we were not mistaken. Now, don't you see how selfish we were to take presents from the School when we had already been remembered by kind friends and affectionate parents?—especially since there are so many thousands of children in this city who have *never* had a Christmas present. If it is not a greater, it certainly is a more Christian pleasure to give to these out of our abundance, than to receive gifts ourselves. I am not going to ask you for a show of hands on this question, for there might be one among you weak enough to say you'd rather receive than give; and that, you know, would spoil the effect of my speech!"

After the Pastor's address followed more hymns, recitations by the scholars, and the usual distribution of prizes for punctual and regular attendance.

The goods were distributed among needy families and schools. Many homes in this city were made glad. Packages were sent through Mr. Spicer, the agent of the American Sunday School Union, to the remote mountain districts of this State, and the Adirondack region. Appreciative letters have been received from grateful recipients and read before the School. In this way have the scholars personally experienced the blessedness of giving. They have seen that self-denial, like " the quality of mercy," *is twice blest!*

It is estimated that of those who have joined the Church of the Strangers, between 125 and 150 have come from its Sunday School. Many others have gone out from the School and joined other Churches.

SUNDAY SCHOOL WORK FOR MISSIONS.

During the first few months of the School's existence a scholar was admitted who was destined to be for many years the chief subject of interest.

Charles K. Marshall, a native Chinese boy, was brought to America when twelve years of age. In 1868 he came to New York and engaged in business, at the same time becoming a member of this Church and its Sunday School. His desire to be useful grew upon him, and soon took the direction of a mission to his native land. He wanted to preach Jesus to his own countrymen.

Through the efforts of Dr. Deems a passage was procured for him by the influence of Messrs. Garth, Fisher & Co., and he sailed for China, December, 1868, in the bark "Jennie," Capt. Cromwell. He put himself at once in communication with the missionaries at Shanghai, where he labored for a season, rapidly reacquiring his native tongue and gaining the confidence of the older missionaries. He next went to Soo-Chou, where he preached and collected a Church. He married a native Chinese, a Christian woman, and sister of a native minister of the Protestant Episcopal Church. She soon became helpful in his work.

To support these two missionaries a Missionary Society was organized in the School. Any person connected with the School became a member by the payment of ten cents a month, and others by the payment of twenty-five cents a month.

: In May, 1871, the Society reported for one year:

Receipts, ...$262.13
Remittances to "Charlie" Marshall, 261.45

Balance on hand, ... $0.68

The School some time after this procured a lot and chapel in Soo-Chou for Mr. Marshall, in which he continued for a number of years to preach the Gospel.

In 1878 the Society was reorganized and transferred to the Church. In another chapter its subsequent history is detailed more at length.

But, though no longer the channel through which the missionary effort of the Church was directed, the School did not lose its zeal for missions. In 1881 it took up the education of a native boy in Bishop Gobat's Protestant School on Mt. Zion, Jerusalem. Christos Tadros, now deceased, learned through the bounty of this school, to speak and write English with creditable accuracy, and gave much promise of future usefulness, when he was stricken down by a fatal disease. His brother, who is attending the "Syrian Protestant College" at Beyrut, Syria, has become the new beneficiary. Following is a copy of a part of a letter written to the School by Christos Tadros, under date of November 4, 1885:

"I had the pleasure of spending my holidays with my mother and brother, at Jaffa, where the beautiful sea is and where there are so many orange gardens. It is over three weeks since our School began again: a great number of new boys have been admitted. Here are some of their names. [The list is written in two columns, one Arabic, the other English, the latter including *Daniel, Paul, Michael, Demitrius, Elias, John,* etc.]

We have not got any rain and our cisterns are all empty. We shall be so glad to have fresh water to drink."

The boy, at this writing, was less than thirteen years of age, and had attended an English school but four years; yet he wrote quite as well as many an older boy, born in an English-speaking land, that has attended school ever since he became of school age.

VIII

The Chinese Sunday School.

I N the year 1883 some members of the Church of the Strangers had answered a call to teach Chinamen in Rev. Dr. Marling's Church, at the corner of Second Avenue and Fourteenth Street. After several weeks of labor there this little band of teachers held a consultation on the propriety and feasibility of organizing a School in their own Church. The subject was broached to the Pastor, who favored the project, but advised the teachers not to withdraw their entire force from the Fourteenth Street School; and to this day two young ladies of the Church of the Strangers teach in Dr. Marling's Church.

By November, arrangements were completed and the opening of the Chinese Sunday School of the Church of the Strangers was announced. There were five teachers* and six scholars. Among the latter were Nam Ou Yong, the Chinese Consul's little boy, and Key, a younger brother of the same official. The Consul has since been removed to San Francisco as Consul-General at that port. While residing in this city, on several occasions he invited the teachers of the School to receptions at his residence, and seemed

---

* As follows: Miss Annie Loomis, Miss Nettie Westley, and Messrs. R. T. Haines, E. E. Minner, and J. C. Westbrook.

to be deeply sensible of the kindness shown to his countrymen.

The conduct of a Chinese Sunday School was soon found to be no easy task. It was agreed therefore to put an experienced worker at the head. Mr. Farney, a student at the Union Theological Seminary, then on University Place, was the first who accepted the charge. The Missionary Society agreed to contribute one hundred dollars toward the expenses. Mr. Farney was soon followed by Mr. E. P. Ingersoll, and he, in the spring of 1884, by Mr. S. L. Gulick, who labored with great success for nearly a year, bringing in new scholars, and in many ways increasing the usefulness of the school.

In May, 1885, Mr. Gulick was called to a larger field of labor, and Mr. J. C. Westbrook, who had been acting as Secretary, succeeded. Since Mr. Westbrook came in charge the School has been not only self-supporting, but has contributed considerable sums for benevolent objects. He accepted the position with some reluctance, as he himself had been a recent convert, brought into the fold through the ministry of Dr. Deems. With characteristic modesty, he ascribes his success largely to his "faithful" teachers —earnest, prayerful, regular, sympathetic—and to the Pastor, whose "genial, hopeful, energetic spirit pervades this as it does every other branch of work carried on by his Church." Once in three months the Pastor meets the teachers at his house.

The majority of the teachers are women, the gentleness and patience of whose character seem to attract the Chinese and to gain their confidence. Nor is this to be wondered at when it is remembered how young men and boys, with a wicked and cruel insolence that deserves Sing Sing, often maltreat inoffending China-men on the streets. No wonder they are diffident and suspicious in the presence of men! When the Mexican Indian was tied to the stake by the con-querors, a priest for the last time implored the haughty pagan to renounce his gods and become a Catholic. "Will the Spaniards go to that heaven of which you have so much to say?" inquired the sufferer; to which the priest assented. The Indian did not care to spend eternity with men so cruel. He refused to go to the Spanish heaven !

Well might the Chinaman of this country say, " If these be Christians, the Chinese gods are good enough for me ! "

The average attendance of teachers and officers for 1886 was twenty-five ; of scholars, twenty-six. It will be seen that most of the teachers have but one scholar. This appears to be the most successful method, although in some cases small classes have been established.

The exercises consist of singing, reading in con-cert, prayer in Chinese or English, catechism—half the School reading a question, the other half the answer thereto—and reading or recitation by the scholars.

The whole number of teachers thus far registered by the School is one hundred and sixteen, and most of these have come from the Church of the Strangers, while some have come from all parts of the country. The number of different scholars taught by the School since the beginning is about three hundred.

On the evening of Easter Sunday, 1886, a very unusual and interesting service took place in the Church. One of the Chinese scholars named Look Quong was baptized. About fifty Chinamen were present and participated in the service by singing some of their favorite hymns—for Chinamen *can sing*, though they are reputed to have no sense of harmony or of perspective. An address was delivered upon this occasion in the Mandarin dialect by Rev. Mr. Jones, a Chinese missionary, and also one in English by Dr. Deems.

What took place the Sunday morning following is described in the words of *The Mennonite*, a paper published in Philadelphia, whose New York correspondent wrote as follows:

" Last Sunday morning there was presented in the ' Church of the Strangers,' of which Rev. Dr. Deems is Pastor, an unusual spectacle. It was the communion season in that Church ; a season which occurs on the first Sunday in each month. Admission into the Church may be had by letters dismissory from any other Christian church, or by ' Confession of Faith,' by which phrase is meant verbal assent to the several propositions of the Apostles' Creed, so called, a formula of faith substantially agreed upon by all the evangelical churches. Upon the occasion aforesaid thirteen candidates presented themselves for admission, some coming from the Congregational church, others from the Baptist, Methodist, etc.; several came on confession, one of whom was a Chinaman. He stood in the midst of the company, a lady on each side of him, the Pastor of the Church and the spiritual officers before him, and an immense congregation standing behind him to second the welcome which preacher and officers extended to those who took shelter in the bosom of the Church. This Chinese gentleman is the first one of his race that ever joined the Church of the Strangers, although the Church has for several years had in its chapel a Chinese Sunday School with a membership of some fifty scholars.

"This is a single illustration of what is going on among Christian churches in New York in behalf of the Chinese. Everywhere schools are springing up, generally taught by women, who seem in this instance to have more tact and wield greater influence than men."

Look Quong has proved a consistent Christian, diligent in business, fervent in spirit, serving the Lord. It is matter for regret, perhaps, that so few have thus far openly confessed their faith in the Lord Jesus Christ. There are a number of difficulties in the way. In the first place, they are naturally diffident, and avoid publicity. To come before a large congregation of people belonging to a different race and speaking a different language is quite an ordeal for a Chinaman, as it would be for any other man.

In the second place, the Chinese, like the Indians,

are very superstitious. By heredity, religion, and education these superstitious ideas have been wrought into their being. They are so prone, therefore, to impute some special charm or saving power to formal acts of worship that it is not thought wise to urge them too strongly to make confession and receive baptism.

On Easter, 1887, the second convert of the School was baptized in the Church, prior to his reception into membership at the following communion. To show the solicitude of the Pastor lest the subject might attach some superstitious efficacy to the mere rite of baptism, we quote the following elementary instruction taken down by the writer during the "preliminary examination" of the candidate:

"A woman is such, not because she wears a gown, but she wears a gown *because* she is a woman. You are a Chinaman, not because you wear the queue, but you wear the queue to show that you are a loyal subject of the Emperor of China. Now, if I baptize you, that will not make you a Christian. I could baptize a dog or a cat. I could baptize the worst man in China, and he would still be as bad as ever. But you are a changed man. Whereas you have hitherto done nothing to get rid of your sins except what you could do for yourself, you have now determined to let Jesus wash away your guilt; and *because* you are a changed man and love Jesus, you are going to be baptized to show that you belong to Him. "

During the last eighteen months some six or

seven of the best scholars have returned to China to visit their parents and offer them some of their earnings. It is not true, however, as it has been asserted, that all their earnings are carried or sent back to China. They pay rent and taxes. In making presents to their teachers they are generous to a fault. They contribute every Sunday a small amount which goes to defray the running expenses of the School, such as books, slates, etc. For nearly two years the School has contributed money for other missionary work. It has aided the Chinese Sunday School Union, the Gospel Mission, and the Inland China Mission. When the public meetings were held to memorialize Congress for the Chinese indemnity, this School came forward and helped to defray necessary expenses. They took great interest in the recent Bazar of the Sisters of the Stranger, and contributed with unstinted liberality. By common consent, the Chinese table was one of the finest in the house.

As showing that the truths of Christianity taught in these schools are not lightly held or readily forgotten, the following incident is noteworthy. One of the scholars, named Lee Chung, left for China about a year ago. Recently returning, he came back to School, and at the proper time arose in his seat and clearly repeated, without a halt, the words: "*God so loved the world that He gave His only begotten Son, that whosoever believeth in Him should not perish, but have everlasting life.*"

The resident missionaries of China bear testimony to the value of the Chinese schools in America.

Many of the scholars have, upon their return to their native land, been very useful to mission stations, inasmuch as, even if not Christians, they remember the kindness received from Christian people, and help to dispose the hearts of their countrymen for the reception of the truth as it is in Jesus.

The following dispatch, recently printed by the press of New York, bears upon the same question, and confirms the above statements:

" The authorities of China have issued proclamations calling on the people to live at peace with Christian missionaries and converts, and explaining that the Christian religion teaches men to do right, and should therefore be respected. The proclamation reminds them that by becoming converts to Christianity they do not cease to be Chinese. 'Know, therefore,' says one of the proclamations, 'all men of whatsoever sort or condition, that the sole object of establishing chapels is to exhort men to do right; those who embrace Christianity do not cease to be Chinese, and both sides, therefore, should continue to live in peace, and not let mutual jealousies be the cause of strife between them.' The change has been brought about without any outside pressure."

IX

Prayer Meetings.

THE REGULAR WEEKLY PRAYER MEETING.

THE prayer meeting of the Church of the Strangers is probably one of its strongest features.

From a well-known work by a distinguished clergyman, we copy the following passage:

"I suppose there is hardly any other part of Church service that is regarded with so little estimation in the community at large as the prayer meeting. And I think facts will bear me out in saying that this feeling is participated in by the Church on the part of the greatest number of its members, nine out of ten of whom look upon it as perhaps a duty, but almost never a pleasure. It is a 'means of grace'; and they feel about it as I did when I was a boy about being washed in the morning and having my hair combed. It was better than going indecent; but it was an exercise that I never enjoyed, and I was heartily glad when it was over. In most Churches I think that is the feeling in regard to the prayer meeting; that it is dull; that it is for the most part without edification; that in some mysterious way it may be blessed to the soul's good,—but how, they do not know."

We are glad to believe that, if this be the feeling in

"most Churches," the Church of the Strangers has the grace to belong to the minority.

The prayer meeting ought to be regarded as the very centre and heart of Church life. The preaching service is very important, indeed ; but in Protestant Churches the sermon is the principal part of it. Almost everything is done by one man. The preacher reads a lesson, and the congregation hear it ; he gives out a hymn, and the choir sing it ; he delivers the sermon, and the people listen to it. But what have the congregation done ? They have contributed their presence. They come to get something, to *get* a blessing, to *get* a sermon. This is all very well in its way ; but if it is the whole of a Church's experience, its members must necessarily be very imperfect Christians. A preacher in such a Church fills an office somewhat similar to that of a coachman or a valet ; he is hired to perform other people's devotions. The service of a Christian is one that cannot be done by proxy : God and the soul must come in contact, or they must remain strangers.

Now, the prayer meeting is a place where people go to perform their own devotions. Here, each one, however feeble, may contribute something. He is not necessarily a mere passive recipient ; he may experience the greater blessedness of *giving*.

In Churches where the prayer meeting is a failure, there is nothing left but the pulpit ; and if the pulpit fails, the whole collapses.

The prayer meeting is the place for Christian fellowship, which, especially in New York, is so rare. We all " believe " in fellowship, because we have so little opportunity of *knowing* it.   One woman is known by the writer to have sat for ten years in a pew behind another woman, and in all that time they never exchanged a word.   At last the minister preached a stirring sermon on Christian fellowship, and at the conclusion of the service the women arose, looked each other in the face, and began to cry.   They saw the sin of such conduct and the mockery of such Christianity!

The prayer meeting develops the pew-power of the Church.   It cultivates a devotional spirit, which is infinitely more important even than mere mechanical activity.   We often contrast "mystical" with "practical" Christianity to the detriment of the former. The truth is that a union of the two is as necessary to real Christianity as body and soul are to a human being.   A mere mystic is like a disembodied spirit; an undevout Christian is like a body without a spirit —a mere machine.   The men of power are the men who, amid all the perplexities and details of a busy life in the midst of humanity, do not lose their spiritual zeal.   The danger of philanthropists in this direction is well known, and is finely illustrated in Hawthorne's character of Hollingsworth.   Every working Church is in the same peril, unless it keep up its connections with that unseen Power which is the Corliss engine of all the machinery in the universe.   The prayer meeting is the Church's Mount of Transfiguration, where Jesus comes to "touch" His disciples; where the inner strength is renewed by communion with

God; where everybody ought to cry out with Peter:
"Lord, it is good for us to be here!"

When this element of devoutness is lacking, all
Church work is useless to the workers, and the organization will sooner or later go to pieces.

That the Prayer Meetings of the Church of the
Strangers have been a source of comfort and delight
to its members—and particularly to its Pastor—we
personally know.

Every six months a committee is appointed whose
duty is to take charge of these meetings. Ordinarily
new members are appointed, who are thus early kept
close to the source of inspiration. One or two old
and experienced members are put at the head. The
committee select topics and print them on a card,
which also contains an account of the other services
of the Church.

This method has worked well in the Church of the
Strangers. There are Prayer Meetings just as good,
where the method is entirely different. The object
to be attained is everything; the means by which it
is accomplished may be safely left to local preferences.
With a good leader any method is profitable. With
a poor leader the best method may be fruitless. In
some excellent Prayer Meetings, no one ever knows
beforehand what topic is going to be up. Whatever
is uppermost in the minds of the people at the moment, is allowed to have full scope and consideration.
The skill of leadership consists in training people
into real usefulness without their knowledge. We
give a copy of the current card used in this Church:

THE
CHURCH OF THE STRANGERS
Mercer, near Eighth St.

OPEN SUMMER AND WINTER: SEATS ALWAYS FREE.

CHARLES F. DEEMS, D.D., LL.D., Pastor.

The Church.

PUBLIC WORSHIP.—Sundays, 10.30 A.M., 7.30 P.M.

COMMUNION.—First Sunday in each month, after morning sermon.

BAPTISM OF INFANTS.—Third Sunday, before morning sermon.

BAPTISM OF ADULTS.—Last Sunday, before morning sermon.

CHOIR PRACTICE.—Tuesdays and Saturdays at 8 P.M. Prof. G. W. Pettit, Leader.

The Chapel.

PRAYER MEETING.—Every Friday evening at 7.45.

MOTHERS' MEETING.—Wednesday following each Communion, 3 P.M., and second Wednesday thereafter.

CHURCH SOCIABLE.—Wednesday following second Sunday, 8 P.M.

YOUNG PEOPLE'S PRAYER MEETING.—Sunday evenings at 6.45.

SISTERS OF THE STRANGER.—3 to 5 every afternoon, except Sundays.

SUNDAY SCHOOL.—Sunday mornings at 9.

CHINESE SUNDAY SCHOOL.—2.30 P.M.

MONTHLY MEETING.—Wednesday, before Communion, 8 P.M.

EXAMINATION OF CANDIDATES.—Monday preceding Communion, 7.30 P.M.

☞ *Every service begins precisely at the hour named.*

OUR PRAYER MEETING.

SUGGESTIONS TO THOSE WHO ATTEND.

1. COME TO THE MEETING WITH A PRAYERFUL SPIRIT.

2. BRING YOUR FRIENDS WITH YOU.

3. READ THE TEXTS NOTED FOR THE EVENING AND MAKE THEM A SUBJECT OF THOUGHT.

4. TAKE PART PROMPTLY, BRIEFLY, AND EARNESTLY.

5. THE LEADER IS REQUESTED TO END THE OPENING EXERCISES AT 8.15, OR EARLIER.

January to July, 1887.

January 7.
Consecration. 2 Cor. vi. 17 ; Joshua, xxiv. 15.
January 14.
Self-Righteousness. Romans, iii. 10.
January 21.
Prayer for Children and the Sunday School.
January 28.
The Uncertainty of Life. 1 Peter, i. 24.
February 4.
Preparation for Communion. Led by the Pastor.
February 11.
Prayer for Missions.
February 18.
Saving Faith. Galatians, iii. 11.
February 25.
What am I doing to save souls ? John, i. 35–46.
March 4.
Preparation for Communion. Led by the Pastor.
March 11.
Decision. Deut. xxx. 11–20.
March 18.
Promise Meeting. (*Let each one read a promise.*)

March 25.

Duty in the Closet.   Matthew, vi. 5–13.

April 1.

Preparation for Communion.   Led by the Pastor.

April 8.

Bearing the Cross.   John, xix. 17 ; Matt. xvi. 24.

April 15.

The Perpetual Presence.   Matt. xxviii. 20.

April 22.

Stewardship.   Luke, xix. 13.

April 29.

Preparation for Communion.   Led by the Pastor.

May 6.

Christ manifested to us.   John, xiv. 22, 33.

May 13.

Prayer for Missions.

May 20.

Come Boldly.   Heb. iv. 16.

May 27.

Children of the Day.   1 Thess. v. 5, 6.

June 3.

Preparation for Communion.   Led by the Pastor.

June 10.

A Safe Condition.   John, x. 14–17, 27–29.

June 17.

Experience Meeting.

Select a promise fulfilled in your experience, with brief remarks.

June 24.

Opportunity.   Matt. ix. 37, 38.

PRAYER MEETING COMMITTEE.

WM. S WITHAM, J. S. KENNEDY, A. B. HOHMANN, GEO. G. HOOPER, EUGENE SHUART, and CHARLES YOUNG.

Seven Reasons Why I Should Regularly attend the Prayer Meeting.

1. *It will honor God.*—"Pay thy vows unto the Most High; call upon me   *   * and thou shalt glorify me." Ps. i. 14, 15.

2. *It will bless my family.*—"His righteousness unto children's children; to such as *keep his covenant.*" Ps. ciii. 17, 18.

3. *It will strengthen my spiritual life.*—"They that wait upon the Lord shall renew their strength." Isa. xl. 31.

4. *It will increase my faith.*—"Faith cometh by hearing, and hearing by the Word of God." Rom. x. 7.

5. *It will encourage my Pastor and my brethren.*—"Many shall see it, and fear, and trust in the Lord." See Ps. xl. 1-3.

6. *It will discourage sinners.*—"And the Philistines were afraid, for they said, God is come into the camp." See 1 Sam. iv. 6, 7.

7. *It will add moral power to the Prayer Meeting.*—"When they had prayed, the place was shaken where they were assembled together, and they were all filled with the Holy Ghost, and they spake the word of God with boldness." Acts, iv. 31.

"Not forsaking the assembling of ourselves together." Heb. x. 25.

This committee are obliged to be present to see that the church parlor is in good order, and supplied with Bibles and hymn books; that arrangements are made for hospitably receiving and comfortably seating strangers; and for the conduct of the meeting. One of the committee is always, at fifteen minutes to eight, to take his seat at the table and attend to the exercises and conduct them, unless the committee shall have secured some other person as leader for the night.

The Pastor is in almost constant attendance, sits where he will, and takes what part he may choose in the meeting. He is, however, appointed by the committee always to lead the Prayer Meeting on the Friday night immediately preceding the Holy Communion, which is administered on the first Sunday in each month.

THE NOON-DAY PRAYER MEETING.

The Fulton Street Prayer Meeting is old and well known and efficient; but it is far down town, and business is moving up. In February, 1887, a number of business men in the vicinity of Astor Place consulted together, and agreed to organize an up-town meeting for at least the Lenten season, which was about to begin. They wanted it unsectarian, and as the Church of the Strangers is independent and un-denominational, they deemed it suited to their purpose. Accordingly they applied to the trustees for the use of the church. This was granted, and the result is a flourishing meeting permanently located in the parlor of the church. Thus is fulfilled the long cherished desire of Dr. Deems, *that services might be held in his church every day of the year.*

During Lent these meetings were in charge of the following clergymen, each of whom led for one week only: Rev. Dr. Wilson, Assistant Rector of St. George's; Rev. Dr. Alexander, of the University Place Presbyterian Church; Rev. Dr. Deems, of the Church of the Strangers; Rev. Bidwell Lane, of the Central Methodist Church; Rev. A. W. Halsey, of the Spring Street Presbyterian Church; and Rev. Dr. Judson, of the Berean Baptist Church.

After Easter the laymen took charge; and the meeting is now of laymen, for laymen, and by laymen. The attendance has been uniformly good from the start, and the general testimony of those who have attended is that these seasons of prayer have been delightful occasions. Nor is the attendance restricted to men. It was at first proposed to have a "business men's prayer meeting;" but it was recollected that many women engaged in the drygoods and other stores of the neighborhood, and many who did their shopping in the neighborhood, needed such a meeting as much as the merchants and their male clerks. Hence it was decided to advertise a "noonday prayer meeting," and throw it open to all who chose to avail themselves of its benefits. There have always been a number of ladies present, and some large employers have agreed to make special arrangements to allow their female clerks to take turns in attending the meetings. Plainly, the Prayer Meeting supplies a real need. To get away from the anxiety and turmoil of business, even for a moment, and lose one's self in the contemplation of infinite strength and goodness is a luxury, a restorative to the spiritually minded, that eases every pain and lightens every burden.

The expenses have been defrayed by the laymen who originated the meetings. There has been no fuss made, no loud appeal for support. Everything has gone on in a quiet way. The bills have all been paid by those who voluntarily contributed.

The following names of laymen were appended to the original call: Robert R. Doherty, assistant editor *Christian Advocate ;* B. J. Fernie, editor of the *Christian Herald;* David A. Burr, lawyer ; O. M. Dunham, manager Cassell & Co. ; W. T. Pratt, manager A. H. Andrews & Co. ; Gavin Houston, manager Thomas Nelson & Sons ; George G. Saxe, Saxe and Robertson ; Frank H. Dodd, Dodd, Mead & Co. ; L. P. Tibballs, toys; W. W. Wyman, of Thomas Y. Crowell & Co. ; John D. Cutter ; William Baldwin, of Methodist Book Concern ; E. B. Treat, publisher; W. S. Holbrook, with Charles Scribner's Sons ; William B. Holmes, photographic materials ; J. A. Richards, with Funk & Wagnalls; G. H. Clayton, with Bangs & Co.

X.

The "Mothers' Meeting."

[This edifying sketch is from the pen of the Secretary of the Mothers' Meeting. J. S. T.]

I N the fall of 1880, it was suggested by Dr. Deems, that such lady-members of the Church of the Strangers as were mothers should meet once a month—as many as could do so—for an hour's prayer and Christian conversation, in order that they might thereby be spiritually strengthened and better fitted to fill the sacred office of motherhood, unto which they had been divinely appointed. The proposition was so favorably received that a meeting was held in the church parlor at 3 o'clock, the Wednesday afternoon following the October Communion, a very encouraging number of mothers being present. During that winter the average attendance was about eighteen, and the hour thus spent was of great interest and profit to the participants.

As most of the mothers were to be out of the city through the summer months, it became necessary to close the meetings in June. When they were resumed in October, it seemed difficult to reawaken the old interest. A few mothers came regularly; others but seldom, and only in fair weather. At length the Pastor offered to meet with us. This experiment failed to produce any marked increase of attendance, but his companionship, his sympathetic appreciation of our needs and desires, his sincere words of comfort and kindly advice, his earnest petitions in our behalf at the Throne of Heavenly Grace, made the hour one of two-fold delight. We who were present each month felt very sorry for the absent mothers who were missing these precious seasons.

The June separation again closed the meeting, and when we reassembled in October, 1883, we elected a president and secretary, who were authorized to do whatever in their judgment should promote the good of the cause. A visitor was then appointed to call upon the mothers who had only been present during the first year. Some said it was impossible for them to come, others promised to return, but for some reason failed to do so. Even the notices from the pulpit seemed to fall to the ground unheeded, and in June, 1884, we closed with the same number of mothers we began with the previous fall,—just seven. Our efforts to make the meeting popular had met with so many discouragements that we then almost resolved to abandon any further attempt to keep it going, feeling that God's time for such an enterprise in our Church had not yet come. Accordingly, when October came again, there was no meeting, only a longing, instead, in the hearts of the few, for something that was more precious to them than they had before realized. Another meeting date passed, and the longing became an actual pain. Then our president said: "Let us make one more trial and let the matter become a subject of earnest prayer with us all. If ten mothers come, we will regard it as a desire on God's part that we should continue the meetings. If a less number be present, we will consider that it is our duty to adjourn finally."

The meeting was appointed for November 28. Trustfully and hopefully, we came together that afternoon, and to our intense joy there were ten of us—*just ten*. It seemed such a direct answer to prayer, such a practical proof of the Saviour's interest in these meetings, that we really *felt* His presence in our midst. We re-elected our president and secretary that day, and each one of us promised that, if Providence permitted, we would attend faithfully all winter. Our Pastor then decided that in the future he would be present only at the opening or the close of the meeting, in order that it might be strictly a Mothers' Meeting, in which the ladies might feel more free to speak. We gave him up most reluctantly, and only because of his arduous labors in other departments. It was also resolved that a mother should be appointed at each meeting to take charge of the next. The leader for January, 1885, suggested that she should select her texts and send them to the secretary to be distributed to the other mothers, a few days previous to the meeting, in order that they might study the subject before coming together. This new departure was universally conceded, after experiment, to be both pleasant and profitable, and was therefore permanently adopted. The meetings were continued without further change in form, and with an attendance of

seldom more than ten mothers, and frequently a
smaller number, until October, 1885. It was then
agreed that we should assemble twice a month—the
first and third Wednesdays following Communion—
and see if by that means we could increase the interest
in the meeting. We likewise adopted the plan of
making all mothers and children, whose birthday anniversaries came between meetings, subjects of special
prayer during that time. The secretary also sent to
all mothers whose addresses could conveniently be
obtained, an invitation to come at least *once* to the
meeting. When June, 1886, came we had forty names
enrolled on our list of mothers, many of them such
interested members that when obliged to be absent
they sent in regrets. We then agreed that the meetings should not close for the summer, as heretofore,
but should continue for the benefit of the few mothers
who would be out of the city only transiently. Many
of those who expected to be gone all summer requested
that the texts and a list of the birthday anniversaries
might be sent to them while they were away.

When October came again, no extra efforts had to
be made to arouse interest. It had not subsided, except in a few cases. Through the winter six new
names were added to the list, and we trust many
others will follow.

During the past eighteen months, we have received
several letters from the grown-up sons of some of our
members, assuring us that it has been very sweet and
helpful to them, in their labors in distant parts of the
country, to know that this band of Christian mothers

in the Church of the Strangers are praying for them. A mother from another city visited one of our meetings and became so interested in them, that she went home and started one in her own Church.

Thus, after long and patient sowing, we find good seed springing up here and there. So, thanking God for even these few visible fruits; for the ineffable comfort and happiness we have ourselves experienced in these sweet communings with our Saviour and each other; and for the numerous blessings bestowed upon us and our children, we take fresh courage and, with Divine assistance, mean to press on with renewed earnestness in our efforts to become more worthy of the sacred office entrusted to us. We shall, as far as in our power lies, endeavor to help all other mothers realize the awful import of those solemn words: " Take this child and nurse it for me, and I will give thee thy wages."

Let all who read this humble little history of the hard and patient struggles of the Mothers' Meeting unite their prayers with ours that it may grow in spiritual strength until its power and glow shall be felt through the Church on earth and in heaven.

XI

The Sisters of the Stranger.

VERY early in the history of the Church of the Strangers it became evident that this was to be a wide field for benevolent operations. Its title was unique. No other Church made special provisions for strangers. Among the various charities none could be found which gave strangers the preference. Many coming to New York not of the emigrant class, but yet needing assistance, hearing of Rev. Dr. Deems and his new enterprise, naturally went to him for aid. The demands upon him increased, and already time, strength, and purse were taxed to their utmost limit, while the drafts upon his lively sympathies were enormous. The Church was young and struggling. Composed mostly of those in narrow circumstances, its charity *offertory* was necessarily small. Some means had to be found whereby the Pastor might be relieved and the benevolent work carried on. Dr. Deems took counsel with a lady, a member of his Church, and proposed to her his plan, crudely formed, which he hoped might be developed effectively with proper energy. She "had a mind to work," but hesitated about undertaking duties where the responsibilities seemed so great. Dr. Deems promised to co-operate and give what time he could in furthering the work. After prayerful consideration, Miss Cecile Sturtevant consented to make the experiment. She entered upon the labors on January 18, 1869. The title "Sisters of the Stranger" was adopted for the work. Meantime Dr. Deems had found a generous-hearted woman, not a member of his Church, but interested in his movements, who recognized the importance of his plans for greater usefulness. This lady, Mrs. H. B. Cronly, kindly pledged herself to support the enterprise for the first ten weeks. Encouraged by this ready sympathy, Miss Sturtevant set resolutely to work in every direction, receiving applicants at her own home, investigating cases brought to her notice, soliciting funds, attending to the correspondence, and interesting charitable people, both men and women, in the cause. Among the earliest to enter heartily into the project was Miss Cordelia Gillespie, now Mrs. E. F. Bermingham, a warm friend of Dr. Deems, and a member of his Church. Ladies from other Churches were attracted, and gentlemen in business circles began to be interested. Confidence was felt in the wisdom of an undertaking in which Dr. Deems was a leader, and which supplied a long-felt want. The efforts made were seen to be judicious. Friends arose. Eight ladies became subscribers at one dollar a month. Another lady contributed fifty dollars.

As the interest increased the work grew. Applications for assistance became more numerous. Within three months it was found necessary to secure an office for the transaction of business. A suitable room was found in the Bible House at a reasonable rent. As yet there had been no attempt at organization, it being thought better to proceed carefully and see what Providence might indicate.

At length it appeared desirable that the ladies should organize for more effective work, and a meeting of the members and friends of the cause was held on the eighteenth of May, 1869, just four months after the initial step had been taken. The American Board of Commissioners for Foreign Missions kindly offered the use of their rooms for the meeting, the office of the " Sisters " being too small for the purpose. By request, the Rev. Dr. Deems presided, and Miss Cecile Sturtevant acted as secretary *pro tem.*

The financial exhibit showed that in four months $140.72 had been disbursed in relief, and that thirty-three strangers had received help. Of these six were from England, five from Ireland, four from Germany, four from New York State, four from Rhode Island, three from Virginia, two from Massachusetts, two from South Carolina, and one from Georgia. The report also showed that in several cases clothing had been provided and medical and legal advice secured without charge. One hundred and thirty visits had been made by Miss Sturtevant in the interest of the Society. This report was encouraging. A Board of Officers was elected for the current year. Dr. Deems was appointed Auditor of the Society. Miss C. Sturtevant was elected Secretary and Treasurer. It was determined that the object of the Society should be to assist strangers in this city; affording temporary relief, so far as practicable, by giving food, clothing, shelter, medical attendance, legal advice, and such general information as might be needed on the subjects of obtaining employment, boarding-houses, and Churches. All the ministrations of the Society were to be given regardless of the nationality, creed, age, sex, or color of the applicant

In the following year it was thought better to re-move the office to the Chapel, 4 Winthrop Place. The Trustees of the Church fixed the rental at $200 a year. This was paid by the Sisters for five years and a quarter. At that time it became necessary for the Church to use this room for the Sunday School. Then the Pastor, with the concurrence of the Church officers, kindly granted the use of the church parlor for the work of the Sisters free of rent, which favor has been continued to the present.

The opening of the year 1871 found the Sisters "faint, yet pursuing." The way was often hard, the means small; frequently cases of pressing need were presented to them when the exchequer was too low to afford the necessary relief; but the money always came at last, miraculously it seemed sometimes. The Secretary well remembers how her discourage-ment was rebuked on one occasion when the treasury was empty and she saw no prospect of money com-ing. It was time to go home, and she was about to leave the office with a heavy heart, when a gentleman entered and told her that he had been attracted by the title of the Society, and wished to make a dona-

tion to a cause so excellent. He handed her twenty
dollars, and promised further aid in the future. The
Secretary went home with a glad heart, but repent-
ing of her want of faith. This gentleman, Mr. J. H.
Keyser, afterwards maintained a lodging house for
men and women called the "Strangers' Rest," where
the Sisters had the privilege of sending applicants
without charge, the only conditions being sobriety of
the applicant, and a thorough bath in a room comfortably fitted up for this purpose. Strange to say,
not a few of the *men* preferred to lodge in a station
house or stay in the street, rather than submit to the
cleansing process! Needless to add, that when one
of this class presented himself a second time for help,
it was not granted.

Mr. Keyser also allowed the Sisters to send their
sick pensioners to his "Hospital for Strangers,"
where they received the kindest care. These institutions no longer exist, but for a long time they were
of great use to the Society.

About this time Dr. Francis Moore became interested in the work of the Sisters, and gave his professional services gratuitously, doing all he could
to advance the interest of the Association. On
one occasion, having a poor family from the South
in his charge, whose children were down with scar-
let fever, he sat more than one night by the bed-
side of the little sufferers, and brought them safely
through. The gratitude of the parents was un-
bounded. Dr. Moore continued to co-operate with
the Sisters until he went abroad. Later he entered

the Church of Rome, and is now a devoted priest doing duty out West.

A Bible Reader having been recommended as an efficient help in their work, the Sisters employed in that capacity for several months, Mrs. Boyd, who afterwards took the position of matron in the " Free Dormitory for Women," which was under the auspices of the " Fraternals," a society of young men belonging to the Church of the Strangers. The Sisters co-operated with the " Fraternals " as far as practicable by donations of money and clothing for the women. Bedding and other necessary articles were also contributed from time to time. Applicants sent by the Sisters received free shelter at the Dormitory. To aid the " Fraternals " in this work still further, as well as for their own accommodation, the Sisters furnished a room in the Dormitory with two beds. This chamber was reserved for their applicants until eight o'clock each evening. This branch of the work was called the " Helping Hand."

In October, 1870, Dr. Deems suggested a plan for the establishment of a " Home for Convalescent Men," to be placed under the care of the Sisters if it should be found feasible. He was moved to this work by meeting in his pastoral rounds, and elsewhere, so many men who had been discharged from the hospitals in New York, because they had been pronounced " cured," but who were too weak to go about the disheartening task of seeking employment. A week or two of comfortable lodging and nourishing food would, he believed, tide such needy ones over their first convalescence and enable them to start out with renewed strength.

Nothing definite was done in this direction until the following year, when it was determined to try to establish a home for this class of applicants. A committee was appointed, consisting of Mrs. Lozier, Mrs. Ogden, and Mrs. Knapp, with the Pastor and Miss Sturtevant. They made diligent search for a house suitable for a home ; but failed to find such. It was then decided to try the experiment of placing such applicants as came well recommended, in families who would care for them at reasonable rates of compensation. Mrs. Lozier superintended this branch of the work. This method of providing for the men was continued for several months, when part of a house on Amity Street was taken. Furniture was supplied by friends of the cause, and the work went on under the supervision of Mrs. Lozier, Mrs. Horne having charge of the apartments. The rooms were held until the spring of the following year, when removal became necessary, and another apartment was secured on Clinton Place. The former matron having resigned, a new one was engaged. She proved inefficient. The plan of maintaining a home was found to be too expensive, and, after due deliberation, was relinquished, and another adopted, which has been in force ever since. Instead of boarding the men in private families, an arrangement is made for them at a respectable lodging house, where comfortable beds and nourishing meals are furnished, the bills for which are paid monthly by the Sisters out of a fund held by Dr.

Deems, made up of special donations for the purpose. $813.85 were expended the first year in caring for 91 convalescents. Among these was an Arab, Madani el Koreichy, who was provided for in a private boarding house during his convalescence. Afterwards, by a special effort, a sum of money, amounting to $91.50, was raised to pay his expenses to his home in Algiers. In the six years, ending Dec. 31, 1886, $2,155.56 was collected and expended in caring for 254 convalescents. The rent of the rooms and necessary supplies for the home rendered the outlay in the first two years greater than in the subsequent four years. Since the lodging house plan was adopted the board of each man has averaged about $4.50 a week.

A new and interesting feature of the work was begun in July, 1883, through a suggestion of Miss Agnes Saunders, formerly an inmate of the Half-Orphan Asylum in New York City. Gratefully remembering the care given to herself when too young to earn her own support, she resolved to devote her summer vacation to a few poor children, who had no other chance for country recreation. In a letter to Dr. Deems she made known her wish, and asked for co-operation. By an appeal from the pulpit the funds were raised, and the Sisters gladly superintended the enterprise The experiment proved a success. Nine poor children had the benefit of seven weeks in the country, with good food, shelter, clothing, and such moral training as they had never known before. The party occupied a cottage owned by Mr. Moody, the evangelist, in Northfield, Mass. It was named

"Happy Home" by Miss Saunders, who found great delight in the companionship of her little charge, a band of lovable and tractable children. They returned in September, well supplied with warm clothing for the winter, and without having had one hour of sickness. Mr. O. L. Johnson, Jr., Treasurer of the Norwich and New York Transportation Co., furnished tickets for the party at greatly reduced rates. The necessary bedding and furniture for the cottage was loaned by the Young Ladies' Seminary, in Northfield, established by Mr. Moody. Special donations, amounting to $149.50, covered the expenses. The enterprise found many friends in Northfield, who sent generous supplies of butter, milk, and other provisions to feed the little ones. These were inestimable luxuries to the children, who were all unused to such things. We are not permitted to mention the names of those who supported this good work, but,—"Inasmuch as ye have done it unto one of the least of these, ye have done it unto me."

In 1884 the illness of Miss Saunders rendered it impracticable to repeat the fresh-air work of the previous summer, but several children were made happy by trips to the seaside, the funds for which were contributed by other children more highly favored, who thought they would enjoy their own country sports the more for having helped some poor little ones to a taste of like pleasure. One sweet little boy wrote to the Secretary thus: "Dear Miss Cecile,—I send you all my money. When it gets warmer in New York, please give it to the poor little children, so they

can play in the sand on the sea-shore and build forts.
Tell them they can pick, oh, so many flowers that
don't belong to *somebody*, and cherries and berries
too. We have lots of berries and squirrels and birdies
that are very funny, cunning, and all kinds. Your
little friend, Everitt Crawford."

The "Hiawatha Club" contributed $200 to the
Fresh Air Fund. This club consisted of eight little
girls from eleven to thirteen years of age, all attending
the same day-school. The president of the club, Miss
Lulu S. Little, moved by tender compassion for the
children of the poor, conceived the idea of getting up
a fair and thus raising a Fresh Air Fund for their
benefit. She consulted her mother, who entered
heartily into the project, and then broached the subject to her little companions. All were pleased with
the idea, and the work was begun promptly and with
energy. Seeing their zeal, the friends of these good
children became interested, and with their generous
co-operation the fair was a success beyond the hopes
of the most sanguine. The little workers felt fully
repaid for their efforts when they found themselves
able to contribute to several charities, thereby securing to scores of poor children a taste of fresh air and
country life. And all this grew out of the heart of
one simple child. "Of such is the Kingdom of
Heaven!"

In July, 1885, the restored health of Miss Saunders
enabled her to take charge of the children selected
as beneficiaries of the Fresh Air Fund. The party,
consisting of eight little ones, taken from some of the

most stifling tenements in the city, were sent to a
farm in Massachusetts, where there was plenty of
room in-doors for every one of them, and everything
needful out of doors for the coveted pleasures of
childhood. These children enjoyed the treat for four
weeks; and then eight others took their places. The
Secretary's report for the summer has the following
account of their stay at the farm:

"What a happy time the little beneficiaries of this
fresh air fund are having! They are in a farm-house
where they have large airy sleeping rooms; their
meals are of abundant, wholesome food; they have
rides in the farm wagon, rambles in the woods, ber-
rying excursions, and frolics in the hay fields. A
swing in the barn is added to their pleasures, and
each day is full of new joys which they accept gratefully, and for which they make what return they can
in good behavior. Miss Saunders is much pleased
with the lovingness shown by these poor children.
To most of them much hardship has come, while but
little tenderness has fallen to their lot, so that to be
exempt from hard words and cruel blows, to hear no
sigh from an over-burdened mother, no curse from a
drunken father, to be well fed, to be clean, to sleep
on a comfortable bed, is to enjoy an existence hitherto
unknown. Thus far they have proved most tractable,
and their behavior in Church has been a model for the
town children, for not one of them has had to be re-
proved for restlessness during service. The pet of
'Happy Home' is a dear little girl named Sadie,
only five years old, and looking much younger, she is

so delicate and puny from lack of proper nourishment. She is a winning little creature, loved by all, and the 'Sisters' hope to have her transformed into a plump and rosy child before she goes home.

"The older girls are learning to sew, and show much aptitude for the needle. When the weather is warm they sit out under the trees with their work and sing with Miss Saunders, or listen while she reads to them some pleasant story. They are so fond of this morning hour that they break up with reluctance when play-time comes. And they are learning still better things: about the Good Shepherd and His love for little children; and although the time for such instruction is but short, it is hoped that the seed thus sown will not be entirely thrown away, but may, in God's good time, spring up and bear fruit."

Among other liberal contributions to this fund, $100 was donated through Miss Edith Little, from the "Lana Ac Tela Society." The young ladies who composed this society, of which Miss Isabel D. Armstrong was president, and Miss Louisa Haynes, corresponding secretary, were school-mates of Miss Little, and with her desired to do something for poor children. So they set to work to get up a fair, and distributed the proceeds among several worthy objects, including that of the Sisters, who were also indebted to Mr. Wm. O. McDowell, president of the New York and Sea Beach Railway Company, for aid in sending families to Coney Island who otherwise could not have enjoyed the recreation.

In 1886 "Happy Home" was again presided over

by Miss Saunders during July and August. Twenty-four poor little waifs had each the enjoyment of four weeks of pure country life. In the roomy old farmhouse they had wholesome food without stint, and comfortable beds, with the delights of cleanliness and orderly living hitherto unknown. Their out-door life was also rich in new experiences, and the children must have carried back with them many pleasant memories to brighten the dreary and squalid city quarters called home. The kind co-operation of Mrs. Brown, Superintendent of the Woman's Branch of the City Mission, enabled the ladies to provide for a larger number of children than they could otherwise have done.

A plot in the Moravian Cemetery at New Dorp, Staten Island, was presented to the Society by Mrs. E. Lonsdale. The first interment was made in January, 1885. A young man, native of Denmark, had been employed by the Sexton of the Church of the Strangers as an assistant, and by his uniform good conduct had won the respect of the Sisters. When his health failed they secured his admission to the House of Rest for Consumptives at Tremont, and cared for him until his decease. They bore all the expense of his funeral. His effects were sent to his sisters in Denmark through the Danish Consul.

In addition to help given to strangers in New York, the Society has occasionally contributed to worthy objects outside the city. For instance:

In September, 1878, $244.60 were donated to the sufferers from yellow fever in Memphis, Vicksburg, and New Orleans. In addition to the money sent, the Society supplied provisions, medicines, blankets, and two cases of clothing containing seven hundred garments.

Mr. Philip Phillips gave an evening of Sacred Song for the benefit of the sufferers, and the net proceeds, $60, were sent to a little girl in Memphis, the only surviving member of a whole family that had been swept away by the scourge. Letters of thanks were received from the Sisters of St. Mary and the Leith Orphan Asylums in Memphis, the Protestant Orphan Asylum of New Orleans, and from Rev. C. K. Marshall, of Vicksburg, Miss. All these were warm in expressions of gratitude for the timely help.

In response to an appeal for clothing, a case containing two hundred garments was sent to the poor of a town in Nova Scotia.

Another case was sent to a destitute family in Colorado.

In September, 1886, the whole amount of the communion *offertory* was appropriated to the sufferers from the earthquake in Charleston, S. C.

These examples will suffice to indicate the scope and nature of the work done by the Sisters.

The Dorcas Committee has been a valuable auxiliary to the work of the Society. The first sewing circle was formed in 1871, under direction of Mrs. A. Simpson. Upon her resignation, in 1874, Mrs. M. E. Ogden was appointed to fill the position, which she has held ever since. The members of the committee meet once a week during the winter months to cut and make garments for men, women, and children. Their fund is derived from members' fees, fines for absence, and donations. The present Committee is composed of the following ladies : Mrs. M. E. Ogden, Mrs. H. Dodge, Mrs. C. S. Shivler, Mrs. E. F. Bermingham, Mrs. A. W. Knapp, Mrs. S. A. Waterbury, Mrs. A. Young, Mrs. J. L. Brady, Miss M. Lee, Miss M. St. John, Miss K. St. John, and Miss V. E. Fisher.

During fifteen years of labor, " Dorcas " has distributed 3,800 new garments, and cast-off clothing valued at $4,000.

The funds of the Sisters have been derived from the subscriptions of members, donations, from various entertainments given by friends, and from bazars held by the Sisters. These bazars have been conducted on strictly Christian principles, and so harmoniously carried on as to elicit the warmest commendations from the Pastor, who believes them to have been a means of grace to all who participated in them. Much of the success of these efforts is due to the assistance rendered by the Sunday School of the Church of the Strangers, the Gospel Mission workers, the Chinese Sunday School, and the Young People's Society of Christian Endeavor.

The Society has an endowment fund of $3,500, which is placed on good security. The Sisters are very desirous of having this amount increased to at least $10,000, the interest of which would about cover the necessary expenses of the work. This fund was started in 1869. Since that time the following

persons have been made Patrons of the Society by
the payment of fifty dollars: Rev. Dr. Deems, Mr.
Cornelius Vanderbilt, Mrs. F. A. Vanderbilt, Mrs. M.
E. Crawford, Mrs. Lispenard Stewart, Mrs. S. M.
Blake, Mrs. Ellen Whipple, Mr. J. H. Banker, Mr. C.
W. Woodward, Mrs. F. F. Chrystie, Mrs. James
Beatty, Mrs. M. E. Ogden, Mrs. R. M. Howland,
Hon. J. Van Schaick, Mrs. H. Seixas, Mrs. E. Lons-
dale, Mrs. H. F. Clarke, Mr. C. N. Deforest, Miss F.
V. Crawford.

In aid of the same fund, the following have been
made Life Members by the payment of twenty dol-
lars: Rev. Dr. Deems, Mrs. Dr. Charles F. Deems,
Rev. W. H. Ten Eyck, Mrs. Ten Eyck, Rev. C. Sans,
Mr. C. T. Smith, Mrs. A. Simpson, Mr. J. H. Keyser,
Mrs. F. F. Chrystie, Mrs. J. C. Tillotson, Mrs. Geo.
Trotter, Dr. Quimby, Rev. Dr. DeWitt, Mr. C. H.
Rogers, Rev. Dr. E. H. Chapin, Mrs. J. Van Ars-
dale, Miss E. Kellogg, Rev. Dr. Savage, Mr. Wm.
S. Bolles, Rev. Dr. Torrey, Mr. J. E. Halsey, Miss
C. Van Wyck, Mrs. H. M. Cronly, Mrs. Beauchamp,
Mrs. B. R. Connolly, Mr. H. P. Smith, Miss C.
Sturtevant, Miss Louise Deems, Dr. F. Moore, Mr.
R. L. Crawford, Mrs. R. L. Crawford, Miss F. V.
Crawford, Mrs. J. Thomas, Miss E. M. Finch, Hon.
J. C. Spencer, Mrs. S. Bland, Miss M. J. W. Simp-
son, Miss L. Halsey, Miss M. C. Chrystie, Mrs. L.
S. Street, Miss C. B. Wardlaw, Miss M. W. Coutts,
Miss H. E. Eels, "A Cuban," Mrs. A. B. Hen-
riques, Miss R. Sturtevant, Mr. M. K. Jesup, Mrs.
F. H. Coutts, General Beauregard, Mr. Sam Ward.

In April, 1884, the Society was incorporated under the Act of the Legislature known as "Chapter 319 of the Laws of 1848." Harrington Putnam, Esq., generously gave his services in securing the incorporation, and begged the ladies to accept the favor as his contribution to the cause.

From the beginning of their work and covering a period of seventeen years, the Sisters have disbursed $23,446.11. They have helped 8,415 persons, and through them and their families many other persons. Of the 8,415 recorded, 4,311 have been Americans, and 4,104 foreigners.

Throughout all the years of the Sisters' work the Church of the Strangers has entrusted to them the disbursement of the Communion *offertory* for the poor. The claims of needy members of the Church having first consideration, the balance, if any, has been allowed to go to the general work of the Society. Whenever the *offertory* fell short of what was required by Church members, the Sisters have made up the deficiency from their fund. The disposition made of this money is reported to the Advisory Council.

The following ladies have been from time to time Presidents of the Society: Mrs. S. M. Blake, and Mrs. Charles F. Deems.

The following have been Directresses : Mrs. Charles F. Deems, Mrs. Jòhn Thomas, Mrs. S. M. Blake, Mrs. H. Seixas, Mrs. E. Whipple, Mrs. Jas. Beatty, Mrs. F. A. Vanderbilt, Mrs. L. H. Keep, Mrs. E. Lonsdale, Mrs. E. F. Bermingham, and Mrs. M. E. Crawford.

The following have been Managers: Mrs. Charles
F. Deems, Mrs. J. L. Graham, Mrs. J. Thomas,
Mrs. R. C. Gardner, Mrs. Jas. Beatty, Mrs. F. A.
Moulton, Mrs. R. H. Johnson, Mrs. M. C. Lloyd,
Mrs. A. Simpson, Mrs. J. Sherwood, Mrs. E.
Whipple, Mrs. E. F. Bermingham, Mrs. E. Lons-
dale, Mrs. J. C. Tillotson, Mrs. A. H. Keep, Mrs.
George W. Clarke, Mrs. Dr. Freligh, Mrs. T. J.
Titus, Mrs. Dr. J. T. Kennedy, Mrs. A. J. Requier,
Mrs. J. Bedford, Mrs. Wm. H. Gray, Mrs. L. Street,
Mrs. S. A. Crane, Mrs. A. H. Elliott, Mrs. Wm. A.
McLaughlin, Mrs. Wm. Mitchell, Mrs. M. E. Ogden,
Mrs. A. W. Knapp, Mrs. J. J. Little, Mrs. J. Ross,
Mrs. J. M. Smith, Mrs. Dr. C. E. Campbell, Mrs. H.
Dodge, Mrs. F. Wheeler, Mrs. C. S. Shivler, Miss M.
St. John, Miss K. St. John, Miss R. Sturtevant,
Mrs. Dr. A. L. Turner, and Mrs. M. E. Crawford.

The work of the Sisters has been carried on unos-
tentatiously, and with as little machinery as practicable.

The giving of *money* has been the easiest part of
the labor. To stir up the sluggish, to encourage the
hopeless, and to impart knowledge to the ignorant,
were tasks far more difficult, requiring patience and
discretion. The peculiar nature of the work rendered
investigation difficult, and, in many cases, impossible.
A majority of applicants had no "local habitation,"
but were often found to claim more than one "name."
Sometimes to refuse instant help might be cruel, to
give might encourage imposition. Much of the work
had to be done directly from the office, if done at all.

Great discrimination was required in order to do justice to the worthy. The Secretary often found her powers taxed to the utmost, and must have given up her position but for the kindness and ready help of her associates in the work. But there were occasions when her own judgment had to decide for or against the applicant. Many a tale of woe poured into her ears would furnish a " Romance " indeed, whether of " Providence " or some other origin !

In a pleasant little poem characterizing the different departments of work in the Church of the Strangers, Mr. George Taylor, a former member of the Advisory Council, thus speaks of the Sisters:

> There are our noble " Sisters," too,
>   God bless them one and all ;
> Their loving deeds, from day to day,
>   Silent as snowflakes fall.
>
> No bright parade nor trumpet tongues
>   Herald their deeds abroad ;
> They move in silence, as becomes
>   The messengers of God.
>
> But warm from many a grateful heart,
>   And many lonely beds,
> The ardent prayer ascends to Heaven,
>   For blessings on their heads.
>
> And while they smooth life's thorny way
>   To many a sorrowing one,
> May each one hear the Master say,
>   " Servant of God, well done."

MRS. FRANK A. VANDERBILT.

MRS. VANDERBILT.

As probably there never lived a man who had done so much for an institution, and so little lorded it over his beneficiary, as the first Cornelius Vanderbilt, so there never could have been in any Christian society a more modest woman than his wife. She assumed no superiority, listened quietly to all suggestions, and was ready to supply the means of aiding projects of others, when commended to her judgment.

On May 4th, 1885, the Society was sadly bereaved by the death of this its beloved first Directress. Mrs. Frank A. Vanderbilt, by her sweet sympathy and unobtrusive benefactions, had won the affection of all the Sisters, and especially of the Secretary, who speaks of her in terms of enthusiastic admiration. A writer in the *Christian Worker* said of her:

"The papers have announced the death of this 'elect lady.' All over the land she has scattered her benedictions, to public institutions, private charities, missions, schools, orphans, widows, aged clergymen, and people in almost every kind of straitness, in mind, body, and estate. She was known to the whole Church of the Strangers, to whom she fulfilled the prophecy, 'Queens shall be their nursing mothers.' 'The Sisters of the Stranger' lose an honored and beloved Directress. Her last words to her Pastor, Rev. Dr. Deems, were uttered brokenly with failing breath: 'I am—going,—*not triumphant,—but—trusting.*' Let that be the motto of the bereaved Sisterhood: 'NOT TRIUMPHANT, BUT TRUSTING.'

" The following lines are from the pen of Mrs. Julia G. Skinner :

"IN MEMORIAM—MAY 4, 1885.

It is meet that the earth should receive her
  In the thrill of her May-time bliss ;
When stirred into fragrance and beauty
  At the touch of the south wind's kiss.

" For earth has a holier mission
  Than gladdening human eyes ;
She foldeth rare germs in her bosom,
  That must blossom in Paradise.

" And, oh ! in the season supernal,
  I think the sweet June draweth near,
The time when God's Lilies and Roses
  Are born in the upper sphere.

" And angels, a-wing o'er the gardens,
  Are pausing in serried array
For grace of a *wondrous white Lily*,
  That opened its heart there to-day."

THE SISTERS' BAZAR.

We are aware of the objections urged by a large body of conscientious Christians against the " Church Fair." It is not our purpose to make light of those objections, nor to attempt a conversion of those who make them. It may not be amiss, however, to explain what we mean by " Bazar," a term which is frequently employed in the preceding pages.

We are not of those who believe in doing evil that good may come. We believe that gambling is a sin ; and it makes little difference whether it be carried on in a grog-shop, on a race-course, or in a church. The thing itself is bad, independently of the motive of the gambler. Whether the gambling be done by professionals for selfish purposes, or by Church people for beneficent purposes, is of little consequence as affecting the moral quality of the act. That which the secular government prohibits in the interest of morality, ought not to be done by the Churches in the interest of charity, and in the name of Christ. We go, therefore, with the most radical in the unqualified condemnation of any " Church Fair " where lotteries are permitted.

What is true of gambling is true of blackmailing. If Christians cannot help the poor or the heathen without a resort to swindling, the poor and the heathen had better be left to perish ; for poverty is not a crime ; and if the heathen lives according to the light that is in him, he may be better off than they who sin against light by robbing people to save him. We have heard of "Fairs " where two or three prices were charged for every article, and where a man's pockets were almost literally rifled if he had the temerity to venture in. All this is not only anti-Christian, it is immoral and indecent.

The Bazar of the Sisters of the Stranger sanctions no gambling, no swindling, and no pressing solicitation. The articles are contributed by the members of the Church, the Sunday Schools, the Young People's Society, and others. As nearly as it can be done, every article is sold a little under the market value. And this is all there is of the Sisters' Bazar.

You may, if you please, urge that the distribution of money so obtained is not Christian giving. We will consider that later. For the present, you will probably grant that at least no crime has been committed. Those who gave their property to the Sisters committed no crime ; those who sold the property for the Sisters at a fair price committed no crime ; and those who gave the money thus honestly obtained from the sale of property voluntarily donated committed no crime. No one has been robbed, no one has been cheated, no one has been wronged in any way.

Moreover, the money is doing the same good to those who receive it as it would have done if it had been contributed directly to the Society.

Granting, then, that no one has been injured, and that somebody has been benefited, two questions remain to be answered.

1. Is the Bazar a *Christian* mode of giving?
2. If not, is it better than not giving at all?

A Christian gift is prompted by that love which a man has for humanity because Christ died for the race. Out of the common Fatherhood of God grows the common brotherhood of man. Christian love is the love of man for Christ's sake ; and Christian beneficence is Christian love at work. Now, any contribution of money, or property, or time, or talent, is a Christian gift when it is prompted by Christian love. No man can tell, therefore, whether property given to the Sisters' Bazar constitutes Christian giving without knowing the motive of the donor. And is not the same true of money directly obtained by collection or otherwise? And, moreover, in either case, the Society is simply the almoner of those who contribute their money or property. The motive is a question for the conscience of the giver. If the almoner contributes time or money of his own he is responsible for the motive of his gift, but no further. In answer to the question, therefore, as to whether the proceeds of the Bazar constitute a Christian gift, we shall be obliged to say : We do not know; but we believe that we have no more right to question the motive of the man who gives *property* than of the man who gives *money*.

But suppose you question the validity of this conclusion. Suppose you admit that the money obtained through the Bazar was honestly and properly acquired, but deny that it constitutes Christian giving; then what? Would it be better not to have given at all than to have given in that way?

To say that the practice of every human virtue is incited by some motive is simply to state the truism that every effect must have a cause. And we all know that among the incentives to virtue there is a wide range. The incentives of the child are not the same as those of the adult. Even among children of the same age a great diversity prevails. A mere request in one case may accomplish what it requires the rod to effect in the other. So among men, the incentives to right action are infinite. One man does right because it *is* right. That is the highest motive. Another does right because he is afraid to do wrong. That is an incentive of a much lower grade; but yet so important is the practice of virtue that we encourage men and children to do right even from poor incentives, rather than do wrong from the best of motives.

Now, giving is a very important thing to the Christian. Jesus was accustomed to say, " It is more blessed to give than to receive." And if there be Christians—babes in Christ—who cannot be moved by the higher incentive of love to give of their substance, we believe it is better that such should give from poor incentives rather than not give at all. We believe it is possible to begin the practice of virtue on low incentives, and as we grow strong by exercise rise to higher ones ; whereas if none but the highest motives were employed, many who now begin in weakness would never begin. In the school of morality and spirituality, as well as the secular school, the studies and incentives must be graded according to the age and previous acquirements of the learner.

If, therefore, it be claimed that the Bazar is only " indirect " giving and not Christian giving, we still believe that even such giving is better than no giving.

XII.

1878.

The Missionary Society.

I N another chapter it is shown that the Missionary Society was originally a *protégé* of the Sunday School. In its early days the Church was deeply occupied with the problem of survival, and it did not make plans for *outside* work until it was able to make ends meet *inside*. Nevertheless, the missionary spirit was carefully fostered in the Sunday School. At least two missionaries had been supported for nine years.

In January, 1878, the Society was transplanted into the Church. The terms of membership were fixed at one dollar per annum, payable annually or quarterly in advance. It was further decided that the payment of five dollars at one time should constitute the donor a Life Member, and of twenty-five, a Patron.

The officers of the Society consist of a President, who is the Pastor; a Vice-President, who is the Superintendent of the Sunday School; and an Executive Committee of six ladies and six gentlemen, who select a Secretary and a Treasurer from among their own number.

Since the establishment of the Gospel Mission, the Chinese Sunday School, and the Young People's Society, each of these bodies is represented on the Executive Committee.

MISSIONARY PRAYER MEETING.

In 1884, a Quarterly Missionary Prayer Meeting, under the joint auspices of the Missionary and Prayer Meeting Committees, was inaugurated. At these meetings special effort is made to cultivate the missionary spirit. Persons are engaged to deliver addresses on appropriate topics. The hymns, the speeches, the prayers, are full of the chosen theme. The Secretary sometimes reads letters received from missionaries; appeals are made, not for present money (though the collection is never forgotten) so much as *fixed missionary endeavor* on the part of Church members. The lack of Christian people is not *means*, but fixed *habits of giving on principle.* Thus a penny a day is certainly no hardship for almost any man who labors. But a penny a day systematically given would amount in a year to $3.65. That this is far above the average contribution of Churches is shown thus:

From the Sixty-seventh Annual Report of the Missionary Society of the M. E. Church (North) the following table of averages per member for the New York Conference, is copied: 1876, 78.7 cts.; 1877, 98.3 cts.; 1878, 64.4 cts.; 1879, 65.2 cts.; 1880, 63 cts.; 1881, 72.9 cts.; 1882, 75.7 cts.; 1883, 73.7 cts.; 1884, 73.5 cts.; 1885, 70.9 cts.

The Protestant Episcopal Church of the United States reports for 1884 a membership of 366,337, in 4,446 parishes. Only 40 per cent. of these parishes contributed to the General Society. The Treasurer reports $271,725 in receipts, which is an average of 74 cts. *per capita*, counting the entire membership, or $1.85, counting only the contributing parishes (Report Domestic and Foreign Miss. Soc., P. E. Church, 1884).

In 1880 [*] there were in the United States about 40,000,000 *nominal* Christians, including Roman Catholics. The amount collected in that year for foreign missions was $2,250,000; for home missions, $2,750,000; total, $5,000,000. This is an average *per capita* of 12 cts.

The same year the Church of the Strangers contributed 65 cts. *per capita*. Four years later, when Episcopalians were contributing 74 cts., and New York Methodists 73 cts., the Church of the Strangers gave $2.00 a head.

The Church expenses [†] of New York City are $3,000,000 per annum. If Christianity lived up to the Golden Rule, New York alone ought, in 1880, to have given $3,000,000 for missions. The whole country gave only $5,000,000. The same year New York's liquor bill was $60,000,000, or $49.70 for every soul! Now, rum is at best only a luxury. It is neither capital, nor any other kind of wealth. It has no claim to be classed among the substantial assets of the community.

If New York gave therefore "as God hath prospered her," she ought to contribute at least $60,000,000 per

---

[*] Van Lennep and Schauffler's *Growth of Christianity.*
[†] Idem.

annum for missions, for that amount represents but a single item of worse than useless luxury.

But during the same year New York spent also $7,000,000 for the theatre, and $4,000,000 for police to keep the rum-drinkers quiet.

All this money that represents the luxury and vice of the community, is given with more or less system. A man goes to theatre a certain number of times a week, or month, or year. The drinker observes still greater regularity. In the morning he takes his "antifogmatic" to get an appetite. After each meal something is needed to stimulate digestion. Liquor is uniformly taken—in cold weather—to keep warm, and—in warm weather—to keep cool.

Even the smoker needs at least five cents a day. Who knows but he gives his Church five cents a week and excuses himself for not giving more on the plea of poverty!

In short, our vices demand and receive *systematic contributions;* what we need is to give some of this systematic and costly devotion to virtue.

As the Church has had thus far only a small fund at its disposal for mission work, it has not attempted to occupy an ambitious field in its own name. The Gospel Mission on Bleecker Street and the Chinese Sunday School are the only such enterprises managed wholly by members of the Church of the Strangers; and the latter of these, as will be seen elsewhere in this history, is already more than self-supporting. The Church has thought it wise to use institutions well and favorably known as organs to perform its missionary functions. In this way the money is handled with almost no expense, is divided into small amounts, which is an insurance against loss, and probably does more good to a greater number than the lump sum could do in one place.

The effect upon the Church of this sacrifice of ambition to efficiency, is to be counted among the benefits of the system. The uniform question proposed by the Missionary Committee in making appropriations has been, not, Where will I get a name? but, Where am I needed most? Where can I do most good? Whenever an appeal has come for help from any source, one thing only was demanded: What are you doing? never: What is your name? So it happens that Methodist, North and South, Baptist, Reformed, Lutheran, Mennonite, Presbyterian, have each applied to the Society for help with equal success, provided their charity appeared in any way to enlighten human ignorance or to relieve human necessity. "All for Jesus," is the motto of the Church. "In essentials, unity; in non-essentials, liberty; in all things, love," properly describes her policy. Members are frequently asked: "To what denomination does the Church of the Strangers belong?" The stereotyped answer is: "We belong to all, and all belong to us."

Let a stranger come to New York from whatever quarter of the globe he may, of whatever name, race, or color, craving human sympathy or Christian fellowship, and he will find *his* Church here; a Church organized especially for him. And there are probably few States or Territories in the Union, few countries on any Continent, that have not some man or woman who has at one time belonged to the Church of the Strangers or worshiped therein.

SOME OF OUR FIELDS.

The Syrian Protestant College at Beirut, Syria, was incorporated in 1863 by the Legislature of the State of New York, and is under the control of a Board of Trustees residing here, who have control of all the general College funds.

The religious instruction of the College consists of regular weekly Bible recitations. There are morning and evening prayers daily, and a regular preaching service every Sunday morning in the chapel. There are also Bible classes Sunday afternoon, conducted by the various teachers.

The Church of the Strangers has endowed a scholarship ($80 annually) for the benefit of Amin Haddad, who has completed the academic course and has, at this writing, reached his third year in the medical department. The College has now in charge another student, recently transferred from Jerusalem, and maintained by this Church.

Bethany Institute, in New York City, provides instruction for women who desire to become missionaries, Bible readers, or nurses. For years the Society has contributed its mite to this institution.

The McAll Mission, in France, is well known to intelligent Christians in this country. Mr. M. S. Berger, its Executive Secretary, preached, in 1883, a stirring sermon in this Church.

At the conclusion of the sermon several persons came forward and made up a fund of $200 for the Mission, with the request that it be used for the establishment of a "Deems Station" of the McAll Mission.

Nothing more is needed to show the remarkable receptivity of the French nation at this time for the truth of a warm Gospel than the success of the McAll Mission. It was inaugurated about ten years ago by Robt. W. McAll, a Congregational clergyman of England. He began in that district of Paris where the old members of the infamous Commune live. The first service was held in a place lately occupied by a saloon, and was attended by forty-five persons. At present the Mission has thirty-two stations in Paris alone, which are nightly crowded, and forty-eight stations located in other large cities of the republic.

The Seamen's Friend Society has its office at 80 Wall Street, N. Y. Part of its work is to furnish loan libraries for the crews of sea-going vessels. A library contains, on an average, thirty-six volumes, always including the Holy Bible, unless it is found, upon inquiry, that the vessel upon which the library is placed is already supplied with it. Accompanying the Bible are other carefully chosen religious books, and a choice selection of miscellaneous volumes. Each library ordinarily has two or three volumes in German, Danish, French, Spanish, or Italian ; the others are in English. The library is numbered, labeled, and placed upon a sea-going vessel leaving the port of New York or Boston, as a loan to the ship's company, every one being receipted, registered, and then assigned to the donor of the funds which pay for it, who is thereupon notified of its shipment. For every contribution of twenty dollars for that purpose, a library is sent out in the name of the donor.

Dr. Samuel H. Hall, the Secretary of this Society, has repeatedly spoken at Missionary Prayer Meetings of the Church of the Strangers. He is full of his subject, and has always an interesting story to tell about Jack and the Coming Kingdom. The Society is an organized effort to use commerce as a messenger of the Gospel. Sailors have peculiar advantages as missionaries, and a sailor once converted never deserts. They are a brave and manly class of men, well worth saving.

These loan libraries have led hundreds of seamen to the Saviour of sinners. Individual sailors, entire crews, and very many officers have been made Christians by this agency. The faith of Christian seamen is fed and quickened by these books. Their use by individuals, and at meetings for religious service at sea, has been instrumental in promoting the observance of the Sabbath. They inform and elevate the sailor mentally. Relieving the tedium of sea life, they take the place of indifferent and vile publications. They change sailors' habits, discouraging profanity and obscenity, and inducing temperance and chastity. As an issue of these results, a ship's discipline is improved by a library; safety of life and property is increased, and voyages become, in every way, more certain and profitable.

The whole number of new loan libraries sent to sea from the rooms of the Seamen's Friend Society at New York and at Boston, Mass., from 1858-9 to April 1st, 1886, was 8,512 ; and the reshipments of the same for the same period were 9,170, the total shipments aggregating 17,682. The number of volumes in these libraries was 452,768, and they were accessible, by original and reshipment, to 324,683 men. Nine hundred and fifty-eight libraries, with 24,438 volumes, were placed upon vessels in the United States Navy and in naval hospitals, and were accessible to 109,530 men. One hundred and fourteen libraries were placed in one hundred and fourteen stations of the United States Life Saving Service, containing 4,104 volumes, accessible to 810 keepers and surfmen.

Of these libraries the Church of the Strangers has provided eight.

The New York Medical Mission is about four years old. It has been several times represented at the Missionary Prayer Meetings by Dr. Dowkontt and Mr. Leighton Williams.

In the Gospels much of the preaching of Jesus is associated with the miraculous healing of the sick. "Great multitudes followed Him, and He healed them all." The Lord sends forth His disciples with the command to " heal the sick and preach the Gospel." As its name implies, the Medical Mission is an organization whose aim is to heal the soul as well as the body.   The gratuitous dispensing of medicines is thus used as a means of presenting the Word to those who could not otherwise be eached.   Dispensaries have been opened at 81 Roosevelt Street, Madison Avenue and Gouverneur Street, 42 Baxter Street, 310 W. Fifty-fourth Street, and one in connection with our Gospel Mission, corner of Bleecker Street and South Fifth Avenue.   At each of these places a religious service is conducted during office hours, so that while patients are waiting in line for their remedies they involuntarily listen to the voice of prayer and the melodies of sacred song.   Sickness prepares the heart for the reception of solemn truth. Imagine some friendless, starving inmate of a tenement, drooping under the despair of wasting disease, suddenly aroused by distant strains of—

> " What a friend we have in Jesus,
>   All our sins and griefs to bear ;
> What a privilege to carry
>   Everything to God in prayer !"

Such a message so borne has won trophies for the Master where ordinary methods had failed.

Another part of the Medical Mission's work is to prepare *medical missionaries*.   The great want of heathen lands to-day is doctors no less than Christianity.   To the ear of Christendom comes the agonizing cry of the heathen world for medical aid and the Gospel of peace.   There are nearly 1,000,000,000 of heathen in the world.   Of these 40,000,000 die annually without any medical aid.   There is one medical missionary to about 10,000,000 of heathen, while in

the United States, there was, in 1880, one doctor to
every 585 persons. A man in New York breaks his
leg and is taken to the hospital, where he receives
skillful treatment and rapidly recovers. A man in
China breaks his leg, and before the doctor comes
it rots off.

The Medical Mission has received much sympathy
and a number of small donations from the Church of
the Strangers.

" *The Tombs Mission* " is a term here used to de-
note the work of Rev. S. G. Law. It is a non-sec-
tarian and voluntary effort on the part of an humble
and useful minister to reclaim criminals to a life of
virtue and a saving faith in Jesus Christ. This clergyman has on several occasions addressed our Missionary Society, and has the entire confidence of the
same.

The Tombs, as every reader knows, is the city
prison of New York. It contains persons accused of
crime and awaiting trial. It is the same "dismal-
fronted pile of bastard Egyptian" that Dickens saw
in 1842. It is among the famous prisons of the
world, and seemed to the imagination of the novelist
" like an enchanter's palace in a melodrama." In the
neighborhood of the City Hall there was formerly a
pond, connected by a strip of swamp running in the
direction of what is now Canal Street. In 1836 this
pond was filled in, and on the site arose, within two
years, a magnificent granite structure covering an entire block, and known, from its damp and unhealthy
condition at first, as the *Tombs.* It is one of the most

imposing buildings on the island; but so unfortunate in its situation that the effects of its grand proportions are entirely lost.

Within the high wall that surrounds the prison on all sides are narrow buildings, four stories high, with galleries running along the walls instead of floors, so that the centre is open from the ground to the ceiling. On each tier are two opposite rows of small iron doors—like furnace doors they seem—but cold and black, as though the fires within had all burned out. Behind each door is a human being deprived of liberty for an alleged crime. Prisoners wear their own apparel, and enjoy many privileges which a *convict* does not share. Over each door hangs a small slate, whereon the name of the inmate is written.

Standing in these galleries, where his voice may be heard by every prisoner who cares to go to the grated door of his cell, Mr. Law may be heard on certain days of the week preaching the Gospel. He does not see his audience; does not even know whether he has any. The majority may scoff at his words; others may refuse to listen. But perhaps there is one whose early life of piety, bringing with it the face of his dead mother, is now recalled by the words of the good man. He is led to repentance. The next day when Mr. Law passes from cell to cell to seek by private interview for the fruit of his preaching, this prisoner opens his heart, the two go on their knees together, and there, on the stony floor, begins a new life in Christ Jesus.

For five years Mr. Law has had support from the

Church of the Strangers. He never begs, thankfully receives what is given, and is content to publish the glad tidings in this obscure and unpromising field, leaving the results to his Master.

The interest of the Church of the Strangers in this Mission may have been originally stirred by the fact that in the beginning of his ministry in New York Dr. Deems had, every Monday morning, for months labored with the prisoners for more than an hour, and had become greatly interested in a work which he continued so long as other duties allowed.

The Hebrew Christian Church (17 St. Mark's Place, N. Y.).—To recount in detail how the late Rev. Charles Freshman, D.D., a distinguished rabbi of Hungary, graduate of the Jewish Theological Seminary at Prague, came to Canada in 1855 and settled down as the rabbi of the Synagogue in Quebec ; how he was led to consider the question whether, after all, Christians might be right in accepting Jesus Christ as the Messiah ; how he was converted ; how he began missionary work in his own family ; how his father, mother, brothers and sisters received the rite of baptism in a Methodist Church, and in the presence of an immense congregation ; how the children, seven in number, from the lad of sixteen down to the infant in arms, were ranged up and also admitted into Church ; all this, we say, were too long for our purpose ; but it is a thrilling story.

One of those children was Rev. **Jacob Freshman,** now Pastor of the " First Hebrew Christian Church in

America." Jacob was thoroughly converted to God.
He began his Christian ministry in a Sunday School;
then he became a local preacher; and finally a
regular minister under the control of the Mon-
treal Conference of the Methodist Church in
Canada.

He yearned to preach to his brethren "according
to the flesh." For this purpose he came to New York
some five years ago, casting himself entirely on the
Lord. Among those who early encouraged him was
Dr. Deems. Beginning in the most humble manner
and obscure places, Mr. Freshman gradually obtained
for himself a hearing both among Hebrews and Christians: convert followed convert; the army of sup-
porters grew in numbers; quarters were enlarged;
confidence of friends increased, and the result is: an
organized Church, in a house of its own, valued, with
contents, at $25,000; regular preaching to Jews every
Sunday in English; prayer meeting on Friday night;
Sunday School on Sunday morning; preaching at the
"Jewish Mission Hall," 73 Allen Street, in German
and English, every Saturday; *The Hebrew-Christian,*
a bi-monthly pleading the cause; and a general
awakening of interest among Christians for Hebrew
mission work.

The Missionary Society of the Church of the
Strangers is a regular contributor to this mission.
But the Church may claim the credit of having fur-
nished more than money. It is very evident that
Hebrew mission work must be undenominational to
be thoroughly successful. The Church of the

Strangers has demonstrated the possibility of Christian unity, and its creed and form of organization have been substantially adopted by Mr. Freshman for his Church. Among the members of his "Advisory Committee" we find Dr. Deems, Dr. J. M. Buckley, Dr. Wm. M. Taylor, Dr. Marvin R. Vincent, Dr. R. S. McArthur, and others.

The East-Side Chapel.—In the month of October, 1878, the plan of a proposed mission and reading-room, to be located somewhere on the East Side, was submitted to Dr. Deems. The result was that, with a fund contributed by him and a lady, a beginning was made at 401 First Avenue. Dr. Deems dedicated the Mission on October 21, 1878. For a few months the work was largely supported by members of the Church of the Strangers. Finding, however, that the entire support of the Mission would be too great a burden upon the Church, and that the society of which the lady referred to was a member refused to contribute toward the support of the cause unless the same were kept independent of particular Churches, the original movers permitted the work to fall into the hands of the "East Side Chapel Society," who have ever since carried it forward. Dr. Deems remained a contributor for a number of years, and many of the members of his Church gave occasionally to the work.

The "Chapel" is at present an important and flourishing institution, located at 404 East Fifteenth Street, N. Y.

In addition to the missionary objects specified

above, the Church of the Strangers contributes regularly to Miss Whately's English School at Cairo,
Egypt ; to the Anglo-Chinese University at Shanghai, China ; and to Bishop Gobat's Memorial School
on Mt. Zion, Jerusalem.

XIII.

The Gospel Mission.

THERE are few localities in the city of New York so full of the pitiful wretchedness of sin as that in which the "Gospel Mission" is placed. .One but needs to walk through this section to hear again the Macedonian cry. The population is a medley of French, German, English, colored, and native elements, whose poverty and squalor are among their most prominent characteristics. And when it is added that their little ones, their young men and women, are compelled to look continually upon the vice and crime that come from saloons and other houses of ill-fame, the need of a mission and the courage of those who go there to work in the name of Christ, will at once appear.

The Mission at first occupied the lower floor of a private dwelling-house at 224 Wooster Street, between Bleecker and West Third Streets. An enterprising Chinese laundryman occupied the basement, and above were two or three families. A sign-board between the windows told the hours of meeting, and during the service a transparency in the window and a lamp over the door invited the passers-by to come in.

ORIGIN.

In the summer of 1885 one of the members of the Church (Rev. Edgar W. Russell, now Pastor of the Presbyterian Church, Nottingham, Pa.), became convinced that he was not doing the work he ought to do for the Master, and proposed to himself, if he could obtain the necessary cash assistance and a suitable room, to organize a Gospel Mission. He waited on the Pastor, laid the plans before him, and receiving a hearty Godspeed, began the work. The hunt for suitable rooms was next undertaken, and proved a weary task. The East Side was ransacked from Orchard Street to the Bowery, and from Grand up to Sixteenth Streets, without success. No available quarters were found whose occupancy would not intrude on the field of some other mission. Then the West Side was scoured and many rooms examined, without satisfaction, when finally those above described were seen. They filled the needed requirements of being convenient to the Church, of non-interference with other Christian work, and of being in a neighborhood that unquestionably needed a Gospel Mission.

During all this time the matter was quietly discussed among a few friends, who volunteered the necessary assistance. It was considered advisable that the room should not be hired until fifty dollars had been promised ; and the promptness with which this amount was obtained was very cheering.

The rooms were taken and the work of putting

them in an inviting condition commenced. They were very filthy—walls, ceiling, and floor as dirty as dirt could make them, and covered besides with pieces of wood nailed in every conceivable position. And then men were found in whose hearts the Spirit of the Lord was, who worked without charge in the painting and other renovation. The rooms soon took on a different appearance, looking clean and bright. Chairs and hymn books were purchased, five hundred circulars were distributed by the young men of the Church, and on June 18, 1885, the Mission was opened by the Pastor, more than sixty persons being present.

WORK.

It was decided at the outset to hold services three times a week—on Tuesdays, Thursdays, and Saturdays; and this has been the order ever since. The rooms were usually open at about half-past seven, and as soon as a sufficient number of workers arrived singing commenced, consisting of attractive hymns, which should either draw some outsiders in or leave some song-message of the Gospel ringing in their ears. At eight o'clock the leader took the chair and the formal service was opened. Singing, praying, and testimony followed. The leaders were chosen from the staff of the Mission, and, occasionally, when some speaker of note could be obtained, a special effort was made to have a large audience.

Outside two young men were posted, who invited passers-by to step inside and listen to the services.

Those who would not come in were provided with tracts.

THE READING ROOM.

As the rooms were occupied but three evenings of the week, it was early proposed that a " Reading Room " should be opened, as a resort for those who attended Gospel services, and as an attraction for others who did not. It was using the intellectual net for those who refused to be caught by the Gospel net. Again friends came forward to help in this work, as they had done in the other. Tables were presented, and from the New York Free Circulating Library came a gift of nearly one hundred volumes. The books and magazines were catalogued, and when all was ready the Reading Room was quietly opened.

THE SUNDAY SCHOOL.

The Sunday after the Gospel services began, the twenty-first of June, 1885, a Sunday School was opened, with six or seven pupils in attendance; and God so blessed the labors of the brethren who were engaged in the work that the rooms began to be uncomfortably crowded. The Christmas Festival of '86 showed to the friends who gathered in the lecture-room of the Church of the Strangers, the great progress that had been made.

NEW QUARTERS.

Early in 1887 the managers began to look for better accommodations. They consulted Dr. Deems, and he encouraged them to go on. They finally found what they wanted at Bleecker Street corner of South Fifth Avenue. By this step the expenses, which are paid by voluntary contributions, were doubled : yet every need has been supplied, and the Mission is constantly enlarging its usefulness. The attendance at the Sunday School averages about one hundred and twenty, and at the week day meetings, sixty, two-thirds of whom are strangers.

SEWING SCHOOL.

A Sewing School for girls was opened on October 2, 1885, and is in charge of Mrs. C. Kalt. A lady, whose name we would fain publish had we authority to do so, contributes largely to the Mission, and provides the material for the little ones to try their " 'prentice hands " upon, with the offer that whatever garments they make shall be their own. The little tots exhibit, with delight and pardonable pride, the dresses made in the Sewing School. The attendance at the School is about twenty-five. Only those are admitted who go to Sunday School and obtain the tickets there given.

FRENCH SERVICE.

Standing outside the Mission doors on the evenings of the Gospel services, the young men found that quite a large number of the passers-by were French, who could speak little or no English. Opportunity offered, and the Committee gave one evening of the week into the hands of Mr. Maurer, an earnest member of the Church of the Strangers, and issued circu-

lars inviting "toutes les personnes parlant le Fran-
cais," to attend the meetings; and some of them have
come, and the meetings are growing.

MANAGEMENT.

The Mission is in charge of a "Committee of Management" consisting of ten persons, a Superintendent, and a Secretary and Treasurer, the officers
being ex-officio members of the Committee. The
Committee and the officers are elected at the annual
meeting of the Mission; and all who are interested in
the work can vote. The needed funds come from
various sources. The Church treasury has never been
appealed to, although the Missionary Society has
made donations.

Rev. Edgar W. Russell, who was instrumental in
founding the Mission, acted as Superintendent from
the opening on June 18, 1885, to August 13, of the
same year, when he was relieved, and Mr. Robert
Scott was appointed by the first general meeting in
his stead. This gentleman served with great ac-
ceptability for sixteen months, when Mr. C. P. Shuart succeeded him.

The offices of Secretary and Treasurer were hap-
pily combined, when Mr. Russell retired, in the person of Mr. Walter Jones, who is still (1887) serving
in that capacity.

RESULTS.

What the results are is known only in part; but
what the eyes of the workers have seen of the pres-

ence of God's Spirit, has been enough to cheer them on. Night after night, at the Gospel Services, the friends can be seen praying with men, and pointing them to the Cross; and many who come in without any thought of Christ, go away rejoicing in His salvation.

XIV.

The Young People's Society of Christian Endeavor.

THIS Society was organized in January, 1886.
Thirty-seven persons signed the constitution
as *active* members, and two became *associate*
members. The former class are those "who believe
themselves to have become partakers of spiritual life;"
the latter, those of good character, and anxious to become true followers of Christ, but unwilling as yet to
confess themselves as such. Within one year the
membership had increased to sixty-nine, sixty-four
active, and five associate.

This division of membership was made to satisfy the
consciences of individuals, and to widen the scope and
usefulness of the Society. Thus, an "associate" member may be just as truly a "follower of Christ" as an
"active" member; but there may be many reasons
which might deter a young person from making a
declaration on such a question. It might be a question of modesty or of doubt; and the expressions
"Christian" and "follower of Christ" have acquired
·almost as many meanings as there are sects of Christianity. In the Church of the Strangers sixteen of
these sects are represented: and while an individual
might be a "Christian" according to one of the special
meanings attached to the word, according to other defi-

nitions he would be entirely excluded. If, therefore, the Society recognized only an "active" membership, many young people would be found in every Church that would be ineligible to the Y. P. S. C. E. But this is an "endeavor" Society, and no one is incapable of endeavor. It is therefore provided that some declare to *have achieved*, what others simply *desire to achieve*.

OBJECTS.

It must be remembered that this Society exists *within* the Church, of which it is a part and function. Its aims are the Church's; its fields and its methods are its only peculiarities. It works upon the young through the young. It is not a social club; it is not a literary society; its objects are spiritual; it labors for the salvation of souls and the glory of God.

The *training* of the members is accomplished by plans and works of Christian beneficence in and outside of the Church, and by religious services conducted exclusively by themselves.

Others are attracted to the Church by the personal efforts of the members among their friends. A number of recent conversions are the result of these efforts. Young people go out and try to interest others in the work of the Y. P. S. C. E., and to enroll them as associate members. The associate membership is a half-way house to active membership. It is the first step in the right direction.

MEETINGS.

The Society has two meetings in each month. The Business Meeting is held on the first Wednesday evening following the first Sunday in the month. The Experience Meeting occurs on the second Wednesday evening after the Business Meeting.

The word " business " sufficiently explains the nature of the first named meeting. The Experience Meeting is sometimes called the Consecration Meeting, and properly so. Its object is not to foster the brazen, wordy type of Christianity, to acquire the cant phrases for giving " testimony," but to bring the members into close communion with Christ. The reading of inspiring passages out of Holy Scripture and praying are far more general than " exhortation " and " experience." Where the spirit of prayer prevails, there good is accomplished. It is a question whether exhortation and testimony always have that issue.

In these meetings both sexes take part ; the young women not as frequently as could be desired, but still enough to give encouragement to a hope for better things. One of the greatest afflictions of Churches is the silence of the women. It requires as much grace in a Pastor to bear the silence of holy women as to suffer the verbosity of some of the brethren. It is among the objects of the Y. P. S. C. E. to develop the latent powers of young and sensible women for modest and womanly participation in prayer meeting worship.

COMMITTEES.

1. During the year 1886 the Society had charge of the regular Monthly Sociable of the Church. A committee was appointed for this purpose.

2. The Prayer Meeting Committee has charge of the Vesper Service in the chapel on Sunday evening. The object of this meeting, which lasts half an hour, is to pray for the success of the Pastor's efforts.

3. The Sunday School Committee, which is a new feature, has for its duties the visitation of delinquent scholars, and such others as the teachers may designate.

4. The Hotel Committee leave at the various hotels on Saturday invitations to the Church services of the following day.

5. The Helping Hand Committee has procured situations for a number of young persons needing employment.

A missionary collection is taken at each meeting, and a sociable is held at the close of every Business Meeting.

RESULT.

What good has the Church of the Strangers derived from the Y. P. S. C. E.? We believe, among other benefits, are these :

1. It has woven bands of attachment between the young people of the Church, and between them and the Pastor.

2. It has borne a part of the expense of preparing a native boy of Syria to be a missionary.

3. It has rendered valuable service to the Gospel Mission of the Church in this city.

4. It has aided the "Sisters of the Stranger" in their charities by furnishing one of the most handsome and profitable tables at their late Bazar.

5. It has increased the power of the Church by increasing the piety of its younger members, and finding fields and suggesting methods for *doing something for the Lord.*

XV

Literary Offshoots.

HYMN BOOKS.

AMONGST the earliest friends that gathered about Dr. Deems in his New York ministry were the sisters Alice and Phœbe Cary. Alice's health was so very frail that she could scarcely come to Church, but she kept herself constantly informed of the progress of the new movement, and was assiduous in creating friends for it. She longed and prayed for a Church building. When the edifice in Mercer Street was opened for the services of the Church of the Strangers, she rejoiced with exceeding great joy. But she was an invalid, and never entered the building until tender hands brought her lifeless body into its chancel.

Phœbe Cary was a wholesome person, of exuberant health and flowing humor. She gave practical help in every direction permissible by her literary engagements.

One day, on a visit to the Pastor's house, conversation turned upon hymn books. Both Dr. Deems and Miss Cary expressed their want of satisfaction with any extant compilation. They agreed in the opinion that there were not in the English language, probably, more than three hundred hymns that ought to be used, and so far as their experience and observation had gone in Churches, there were not three hundred that ever were used in the course of a year in any single congregation.

Phœbe Carey banteringly said, "Let us make the model hymn book," and Dr. Deems agreed. His own account of it is, that after they had entered upon the work, both Miss Cary and himself came to the conviction that making a hymn book was no child's play.

Their plan was to have only three hundred religious poems, and that these should be divided into hymns and spiritual songs and lyrics. It was agreed that each "hymn" should be a metrical address to God, and that the phrase "spiritual songs" should have some latitude of signification, embracing whatever might be edifying in social singing, and that among the "Psalms" should be admitted many such as should more usually be "said" than "sung."

To the best of their knowledge, judgment, and taste, first of all, one hundred best hymns were selected according to three characteristics. viz.: (*a*) their poetical excellence, (*b*) their devotional fervor, and (*c*) their popularity. Sometimes one of these characteristics was so manifest as to secure a verdict in the absence of the two others. But in no case was there admitted a hymn which the compilers did not believe to be in accordance with the mind of the Spirit as set forth in the Word of God ; not one that might not be sung in all its parts by all people in the service of the Sanctuary ; and nothing was considered a hymn that was not a direct address to God.

Amongst the "spiritual songs" were inserted some which got their place on account of their popularity. The compilers did not choose to let their standard pronounce final judgment against what thousands had found edifying or pleasant; but in no case did they allow that feeling to secure the admission of what would seem offensive to pure taste.

The third department, called "lyrics," contains a number of poems which can hardly be sung in a congregation, but are profitable for reading; such as Montgomery's "A poor wayfaring man of grief;" Dr. Holland's "Heaven is not gained by a single bound;" Adelaide Procter's "Judge Not;" Jean Ingelow's "O God, O Kinsman loved, but not enough;" Christina Rosetti's "Therefore, O friend, I would not if I might;" Dr. Bonar's "'Tis first the true, and then the beautiful." By observing the canons they had set for themselves, and exercising extreme care, and examining over twenty thousand lyrics in several languages, the compilers produced a book which is believed by many to be the best collection, on the whole, in the English tongue. It has been adopted in several congregations, and will suit for worshipers of any denomination. It was intended that there should be no hymn which any Christian could not use, either in the regular Church worship, in social service, or in the closet. And hence the compilers believed that the name, "Hymns for all Christians," was appropriate for their book. The work was mainly done at the Cary residence, 53 East Twentieth Street, where the compilers had the daily aid of Alice's delicate taste. The notes were all prepared by the Pastor.

Some years after its appearance Dr. Deems wrote to Mr. Whittier for an original hymn for the *Sunday Magazine*, which he was then editing. Mr. Whittier wrote back stating that a hymn was the most difficult species of poetical composition. He said, " *There are not more than twenty first-rate hymns in the English tongue, and thee hast them all in thy collection.*"

"THE CHRISTIAN WORKER."

In January, 1881, was issued the first number of the *Christian Worker*, an eight-page illustrated paper, which attracted much interest. It was edited and published by Mrs. Sarah Keables Hunt, to whom, in the midst of her literary labors, it had occurred that there might be a place for such a periodical on Christian work. In the second year of the "Worker's" life the Church of the Strangers and also the Sisters of the Stranger engaged departments in its columns, for monthly reports of the progress of the Church and the Society, and now the center of its influence seems to be in this Church and its work, though news from other associations are often welcomed to its columns.

Although its pilôt feels that it is only a little bark on a sea of great and noble ships, yet it has carried many a precious message and accomplished much good, and we believe that we echo the wishes of many a fellow-traveler when we bid it **Godspeed** and a long and useful journey.

THE "DEEMS BIRTHDAY BOOK."

In 1882 a handsome volume appeared under the title of *Deems Birthday Book.*

Mrs. Sara Keables Hunt, the editor of the *Christian Worker*, had gathered together many extracts from Dr. Deems's sermons, and thinking rightly that they deserved a place and name, she arranged and edited them in book form, with a selection for every day in the year, accompanied by a space on the opposite page for autographs.

The picture of Dr. Deems, which Mrs. Hunt had made for the book, shows him in one of his most genial moods, and is very appropriate for the pretty volume. It is believed that many who have never been able to enter the Church of the Strangers have been won to pray for its success through the influence of the Deems Birthday Book, as it goes from heart to heart, and from home to home.

LECTURES.

In 1883 the Church founded an Annual Course of Lectures. The object of this movement was to provide for its own people, at moderate cost, intellectual entertainment of the highest character. The initial course was supplied by Prof. C. A. Young, known throughout the world as an eminent authority on astronomy. Prof. Young is seldom tempted to leave his great telescope at Princeton College for the lecture platform; but at the invitation of Dr. Deems, who is his warm personal friend, he consented to appear six nights in the Church of the Strangers on successive Tuesday evenings, beginning with January 2, 1883. Each lecture was fully illustrated by stereopticon views, many of which, together with verbatim re-ports of the lectures, were reproduced on the succeed-ing mornings by the *New York Tribune*. At the con-clusion of the course the entire series was revised by the author himself, and issued in the form of a *Tri-bune Extra*, to take a permanent place with the scien-tific literature of the country.

Course tickets were sold at $2.50 each; reserved seats at $3.00; single tickets (reserved), seventy-five cents; admission, fifty cents. The popularity of the lectures is attested by the fact that the course netted the Committee between three and four hundred dollars.

The subjects discussed by Prof. Young were as follows:

1. CELESTIAL MEASUREMENTS; including an ac-count of the Transit of Venus of Dec. 6, 1882.

2. THE SUN; its spots; its peculiarities of heat and light, etc., etc.

3. THE MOON AND ECLIPSES; the moon's influence upon tides and storms; the growth of vegetation; human life, etc.

4. THE PLANETARY SYSTEM.

5. METEORS AND COMETS.

6. FIXED STARS AND NEBULÆ; why do some stars twinkle? the immensity of the universe; the dimin-utive earth.

Below we give the courses for the succeeding years to date.

1884.

Jan. 9. George Kennan, OUR LIFE IN SIBERIA.

Jan. 16. Prof. A. A. Starr, WONDERS OF THE MICROSCOPE. Illustrated.

Jan. 23. W. J. Marshall, AN EVENING IN WONDERLAND. Illustrated.

Jan. 30. Prof. Wm. Libby, Jr., GLACIERS. Illustrated.

Feb. 6. Charles F. Deems, D.D., EGYPT. Illustrated.

Feb. 13. Phœbus W. Lyon, TRAVELS IN AFRICA.

1885.

Jan. 7. Robert J. Burdette, PILGRIMAGE OF THE FUNNY MAN.

Jan. 14. Helen Potter, READINGS AND IMPERSONATIONS.

Jan. 21. Geo. Kennan, VAGABOND LIFE IN EASTERN EUROPE.

Jan. 28. Rev. E. P. Thwing, Ph.D., RAMBLES IN SPAIN.

Feb. 4. Prof. D. S. Holman, MOTION AND LIFE AS SEEN WITH THE MICROSCOPE. Illustrated.

Feb. 11. Wm. I. Marshall, COLORADO. Illustrated.

1886.

Jan. 5. Charles F. Deems, D.D., REMINISCENCES OF TRAVELS IN THE EAST.

Jan. 12. Rev. John Paul Egbert, Buffalo, N. Y., THE UPWARD STRUGGLE OF THE SPANISH PEOPLE.

Jan. 19. Howard Henderson, D.D., LL.D., THE HERESIES OF THE HEART AND OF HISTORY.

Jan. 26. Mr. M. J. Verdery, LOVE'S LABOR LOST.

Feb. 2. A. H. Bradford, D.D., Montclair, N. J., A JERSEYMAN AMONG THE WEBFEET.

1887.

Jan. 4. Prof. Garrett P. Serviss, HOW WORLDS ARE MADE.

Jan. 11. Dr. W. H. Milburn, WHAT A BLIND MAN SAW IN WASHINGTON FORTY YEARS AGO.

Jan. 18. Rev. Dr. Deems, SOME PEOPLE I HAVE MET.

Jan. 25. Frank E. Hipple, Esq., THE LAW OF CONTRACTS.

Feb. 1. Rev. Dr. Deems, SOME OTHER PEOPLE I HAVE MET.

Feb. 8. Rev. Edward M. Deems, WALKS IN SCOTLAND.

In 1887 the Lecture Committee abolished admission charges, and advertised a course of free lectures. Collections were taken up, however, which in some cases about covered the cost of the lectures. With an occasional donation by some friend of the cause, the free lectures are thus seen to become not only a possible, but a probable, feature of the Church.

THE LIBRARIES.

Four distinct libraries, with as many different uses, are in the Church. One belongs to the Sunday School, and is in the chapel. Another is a technical library belonging to the Pastor, and is in the study. The third is a popular library for the use of the Church members, and is in the parlor. The time to obtain books from this is Friday evening after the Prayer Meeting.

A fourth library has just been begun. Twice a year collections are taken for " Religious Literature." This fund purchases Bibles, hymn books, etc., for the Church, and provides other religious publications for distribution. A card is placed on each book requesting the reader to pass it on. The name and address of the donor are also stated, with a request that if any are benefited a line may be sent to the giver of the book. Contributions are solicited to increase the number of books thus sent out.

XVI

Minor Miscellanies.

I. SPECIAL COLLECTIONS.

THIS being a free Church, the collections are its only source of revenue. As it is widely advertised as the " Church of the Strangers," a great many people imagine that one of its chief functions is to give financial aid to strangers; and therefore the Pastor is besieged by persons from every part of the world, who ask for special collections. The " Sisters of the Stranger " render material aid to the needy, but no collections are ever taken for any of these applicants. Frequently, indeed, after some great calamity, like the Michigan fires, the Western floods, or the Southern earthquake, "special donations" are received and forwarded. The fixed charges and other expenses of the Church are such as to require a strict adherence to the rule above specified.

During the year, however, four "special collections" are taken. Two of these are devoted to missions, and the other two constitute the *religious literature fund* mentioned in a previous chapter.

2. THE SOCIABLES.

On the second Wednesday after each communion a Sociable is held in the parlors of the church, under the auspices of a committee of seven appointed for that service. Entertainment is provided in the form of music or elocution. About half the evening is devoted to social intercourse. Seats are arranged in a peculiar manner, so as to bring the occupants face to face in groups. At the end of each performance it is often humorously insisted that the audience shall " mix," which means that every person in the room is to change his seat. In the course of an evening this method brings nearly everybody in contact with everybody else.

The Committee are expected to be early on hand, to introduce strangers as they arrive, and provide seats for all. They are everywhere present to see that no one is neglected, and that the meeting shall not *drag.* The Sociable is not meant to be a mere entertainment where people go to hear music and criticise dress, but an evening of Christian fellowship. In a city like New York, where people do not know who lives in the next house, something of this sort must be had to keep the Churches from becoming literally Churches of *Strangers.*

Once a year the Committee provides a strawberry festival, to which admission is charged. In this way a small fund is often accumulated for benevolent objects. Thus the Committee of 1885 retired with fifty-five dollars, which they divided between several local missions.

Some of the entertainments given by this Committee have been of the highest order. Readers and musicians of world-wide reputation have entertained the members of this Church.

3. THE STORY OF A GLASS DOOR.

After a season of hard times, which had brought
extreme poverty to many an humble home, a young
woman found herself in utter destitution. Since the
death of her parents, years before, she had managed,
by incessant industry, to maintain herself until the·
financial crisis stopped her work, and rendered useless
all her efforts to find any labor whereby she might earn
her daily bread. One by one she had parted with
her garments, until there remained scarcely necessary
clothing, and at last, in arrears for board, with no means
of payment, she had been turned into the streets of
New York, homeless and friendless. All that bleak
day she had wandered about. Never having asked for
charity, she knew not where nor how to apply. And
now night had fallen—Sunday night—and she had no
place of shelter. Pinched with cold, faint from hunger,
footsore and weary, hope died within her. In absolute
desperation she resolved to put an end to the life which
seemed to have no promise of good for her, but was
full of dark threatenings, like the angry sky overhead.
As she went on through a side street, gaining courage
at each step for the final plunge which would, she
thought, end all her·misery, her attention was arrested
by a bright light shining out on the obscurity. Me-
chanically moving on toward the light, she at length
stood before a church whose outer doors were spread
invitingly open, and whose inner door was of sheet
glass, so clear that the light from within streamed
through without obstruction, flooding the pavement,

and shining far into the darkness beyond. The incident was a slight check to the mad impulse that had
urged her on to self-destruction. The light seemed to
promise warmth, and she was so cold. Involuntarily
she stepped into the vestibule and drew near to the
crystal door, through which she could see a throng of
men and women who were listening to a voice, whose
tones reached her ear; but whose words had no meaning for her dulled brain. But the voice was earnest
and kind, and, irresistibly attracted, she slipped noise-
lessly in and dropped into a seat in a remote corner.
For a while her great wretchedness prevented any
comprehension of what the preacher was saying, but
his voice soothed her, and gradually the tension of
bitter feeling relaxed, and she listened.

The preacher told of the wondrous love which led
the majestic Son of God to leave the brightness and
glory of the Father's house, and dwell among men.
She heard how the Divine One suffered from cold
and hunger, how He was forsaken of friends, and had
not where to lay His head. How He went about doing good, and, worn with travel, forgetful of the wants
of His own humanity, stood with arms outstretched
to the toiling men and women who gathered about
Him, pleading, with eyes full of tender, sympathizing
love, "Come unto Me, all ye that are weary and
heavy laden, and I will give you rest." Then the
preacher went on to tell of the rest that remains for
the people of God; he dwelt in tones of rapturous
faith on the mansions in the Father's house which the
dear Saviour has gone to prepare for His humble,

patient followers; and, as his voice bore the words of
promise to her heart, the ice which had gathered
there melted into blessed tears, and new hope sprung
up and better impulses stirred within her.   She
prayed for strength to struggle on and bear her
dreary life until in God's good time He should release her.   When the congregation dispersed, she
went out again into the cold and darkness, but with
renewed courage and better resolves.   In her agita-
tion she took no note of the street she was on, and
knew neither the name of the church nor of its
Pastor.

Several months later the girl met with a Christian
woman, to whom she confided the sad story of her
former wretchedness and terrible temptation.   She
dwelt on her rescue in words of loving gratitude to
God, and toward the minister whose voice had induced her to give attention to the Word of Life.   The
church whose open doors and cheerful light had
drawn her in and sheltered her until she gathered
strength to resist the tempter, she had never since
been able to find.   Now she had regular employment
and was prospering; she longed earnestly to make a
thank offering in the sacred edifice which had been
instrumental in saving her.

Her new friend heard her story and kindly invited
her to go with her to hear her Pastor.   The invitation was gladly accepted, and they went together.
As they entered the vestibule the girl was struck
with the familiar appearance of a glass door, through
which the light was pouring.   Agitated by the flood

of memories which the sight brought up, she took her seat just as the preacher rose and commenced speaking. At once she recognized the voice, and, turning to her companion, she whispered, while happy tears coursed down her cheeks, "It is he! it is he!"

She was in the Church of the Strangers. The preacher was Dr. Deems. It was here she had found refuge from the storm of fiercest temptation—his was the voice that had called her back from an untimely end. At last she had found what she had so long sought, and her heart was filled with joy and thankfulness. Through God's great goodness she not only had a comfortable home with friends, wherein to rest at the close of each day's labor, but now she has a Sunday home, where she goes to offer thanksgiving and gain spiritual strength.

The history of the glass door, as it was told to the writer of this simple story, is this: Dr. Deems once remarked from the pulpit that he wished the entrance to his church might be made as attractive as the entrances to the various places of amusement. He could see no reason why the house of God should be dark and uninviting, while the haunts of Satan were so alluring. He also said that if he had the means he would remove the heavy doors which shut in the congregation and replace them with glass, which would allow the light from within to shine out on passers-by. Amongst his hearers was Mr. Elisha Sniffen, who in the course of the next week waited on the Doctor, and generously offered to carry out his wishes. The offer was gratefully accepted, and in a few days the glass door replaced the door of wood—with what result in one case, several years after, we have tried to show ; and if the story induce any one to improve the dark and repulsive looking fronts of other churches, it will not have been told in vain.

4. REPAIRS.

Within the last few years improvements involving an outlay of about four thousand dollars have been made *and paid for*, so that the Treasurer, in his last Annual Report, was able to say that every known financial obligation of the Church had been satisfied to date.

The main edifice was roofed, carpeted, painted, and otherwise improved. The Sunday School room and the church parlor were also neatly painted.

The latter is removed from the Greene Street entrance by an ante-room extending across the entire width of the building. A partition and door, formerly both without windows, separate the parlor from the anteroom. An open door and a flickering gas jet within were the only objects that hitherto attracted the attention of the passer-by. One Sunday morning Dr. Deems happened to refer to " The Story of a Glass Door." and remarked that he wished a similar improvement might be made at the Greene Street entrance of the church. At the close of the service a gentleman stepped up to the Pastor and offered a check to pay for the desired change. Carpenters were at once set at work, and now the open door at 4 Winthrop Place no longer reveals merely a blank wall. A flood of light pours through a large window, and invites the passing stranger to tarry.

5. A LETTER.

[On the 6th of January, 1886, the following letter appeared in the *Christian Advocate*, Raleigh, N. C., edited by Rev. F. L. Reid. It was written by a cultivated young lady of North Carolina, who was a member of our congregation while she was studying art in New York.—J. S. T.]

" I attended my first service in a New York church a few weeks ago, and though this may have often been written about, I felt as if a North Carolinian's impressions might interest, and perhaps do good, by suggesting some new methods.

" What church, or society of any kind, can keep *alive* by running in the same old ruts forever? The Pastor of the church in question is alive to his work; his whole soul and body are in it. His chief end and aim in life, I think, are to help those who need help, and by a perfect system he accomplishes about the average work of—how many men shall I say?

" He doesn't do all this work in person, but through him it is done. He organizes this body, that society, begins a library, suggests this or that work to his members, and they carry it on—gives as many as he can actual work. I notice, too, that he has congregational singing. I never saw a church where so many people sung—the children, the young people, and the old. The good attention of all is also marked. There is perfect quiet and order after the services begin, and all seem interested in what is being said. Well, the chief reason of all this is, I think, because he always has something to say, and studies to say it in an interesting and striking way, and tells it as a message for each individual present. Do not let me be understood now as finding fault with the way *we* do things down South, for I blow the Southern horn loudly up here, but I do think that we can put fresh spirit and life into some of our churches by adopting, as far as practicable, some of their methods. I know a church, for example, in which the Pastor, who is a Southern man, makes it his duty to conduct every prayer meeting, *none* of the members taking any part that I have ever seen, except in the singing—not all in this. If the Pastor is called out of town, or is necessarily absent, which is seldom, the notice is given out that there'll be no prayer meeting, when there are Christians enough in the Church to carry on a dozen prayer meetings. Last Sunday evening I attended a prayer meeting conducted entirely by the young men. They meet at a quarter to seven to pray for the Pastor, and a blessing on the night service. Ministers who feel that their congregations are cold, and not in sympathy with them, can appreciate this, and understand what a blessing and help it must be to the Pastor. On the evening of which I speak, a boy led, who couldn't have been over eighteen, but he did what was to be done promptly and with ease. There is little time lost in any of these meetings, and they always begin at the minute appointed, and close at the minute for closing. In

New York time is lost neither in business nor religion.

" The leader calls for some one to lead in prayer—
all bow, and some one rises immediately. This evening another led; without being asked individually, he
offered an earnest prayer that seemed to come right
from the heart. The minute, almost the second,
the prayer is over, 'No. 19, please,' or 'No. 40,
please,' comes from any one in the meeting, and truly
all sing heartily and cheerfully, so that every one
feels that he or she takes part, and has a right to take
part. I think this is what the young people of our
church need, *active work*, that they may feel that
they are *doing* something, and then they will not always be questioning their conversion, wondering if
they are Christians, and always in doubt because
they haven't that religious experience they desire.
It is just at times when we have nothing to do, and
feel that we are doing no good, that the tempter
does his work, and makes us miserable.

" It is all well enough to talk about doing well
your home duties and attending to your daily business, and that this is Christian work ; so it is—but
there ought to be church work of some sort for every
member, so that each member may feel that he has a
right to say ' my church.' The minister or older
members may say or preach that they may, can, or
must do or have such work, and yet not plan defi-
nitely some work and give it to them to do. You'll
find that nine churches out of ten have no young
people's organizations. Young people must be led,

they are babes in Christ, and unless fed and cared for
by those of strength, they will either die in their in-
fancy, or always be weak and deformed Christians.
I am not very old, and I know from experience
whereof I speak, and there is a need for young
people's work in prayer meetings, Sunday School,
societies of all sorts, missions, libraries, Y. M. C. A.,
and Y. W. C. A. The latter I never knew in the
South. It need not be additional work for the Pastor ; on the contrary it will lift some, yes, a great deal
of the burden that weighs him down. The simple
fact of the hearty co-operation of his members
will lighten his labors and cheer his heart. There
are connected with the church spoken of, so far as I
have been able to find out, fifteen organizations—
some for children, some for the young, and some for
the old. The meetings of all these the Pastor
couldn't, of course, and doesn't attend regularly,
though he gets around pretty often ; but he has his
eye, hand, and heart on them all ; knows just what
they are doing, is always ready to advise, or devise
some new plan to keep up a warm interest in the
work. There is nothing, you know, that is so opposed to success, be it in religion, business, or pleasure, as dull monotony. To prevent this, as much
diversity as is possible and profitable is brought in
the services ; for instance, in the Friday night prayer
meetings there is one night called the 'promise
night,' in which any one reads from the Bible some
promise ; one night is devoted to special prayer for
the Sunday School ; one for the young men ; one to

missionary work; and the one previous to the Sunday on which the Lord's Supper is administered is led always by the Pastor, so that he may prepare the minds and hearts of his people to rightly receive it. In this way the interest of the meetings is kept up, and they don't become dead. The last missionary prayer meeting was especially interesting. There was ' a man of Tarsus ' present, a young man who is studying here to go back as a missionary, I suppose. He told us of how he had been treated as a young minister in his country, how he had been stoned, beaten, and driven from their cities, and brought before rulers, as was Paul, and like Paul he found His grace was sufficient.

" Of these fifteen organizations mentioned one is the Chinese Sunday School, and though *we* can't have such a school, for the want of Chinamen, yet there are a plenty of natives, who are, perhaps, as badly in need of missionary work. This meets in the afternoon, and I went round to visit the school, just to see how they did, and what they did ; but the Superintendent came round and said they were in need of teachers, and wouldn't I have a class ; and though I didn't show any special anxiety for one, he went off and soon came back with ' my Chinaman.' One constitutes a class (and this is sometimes more than you can well manage). Most of these Chinese can read in their own language (mine can't), so they have books in which the same thing is written in both languages, and in this way, while they are pronouncing the English words, they can understand their meaning. They seem very anxious to learn, and mine was delighted to write his name. They are certainly curious looking creatures in their careless dress, and to one seeing them for the first time they all look alike. Those who know them well say they are very quick and intelligent. At this school's anniversary this week the Chinese Consul made a short address in his own language, and it was interpreted in good style by his attendant. There are many other schools of this kind in the city.

"One scheme of this church, which strikes me as especially conducive to drawing the congregation nearer together, is what they call their twelve tribes. Members are received into the church every month of the year—hence, twelve times; all who join in January belong to one tribe, all in February to another, and so there are twelve tribes. Each tribe has its patriarch and scribe. Each meets annually the night after the communion of the month in which its members joined, to welcome the new members; it also meets once a year at the residence of the Pastor, and at other times at the houses of the members. Each patriarch looks especially after his tribe, keeps their addresses, so as to inform them of any church movement, and in this way the whole membership is looked after, and each individual feels that he is personally remembered.

"On the first Sundays in June and December they have 'Rallying Communion,' when a special effort is made to bring out all the membership to communion, just before the rest and pleasures of summer vacation, and the hard work of winter. The Pastor calls his discourse 'A Communion Meditation,' and takes some tender topic connected with the Saviour. The communion is like a glad family meeting, in which their love for their Saviour and for each other is increased.

" These are not all the plans of work, but enough to show how, by skillful management, a lively interest may be kept up throughout the whole church."

6. THE CHOIR.

On page 218 reference is made to the devotional character of a choir rehearsal which took place in the Church parlor. It is proper to state that in this Church no one is admitted into the choir who is not known to possess good moral character in addition to a knowledge of music. Since May, 1872, the choir has been in charge of Prof. G. W. Pettit, who was also for many years Superintendent of the Sunday School of the Church. It is a select chorus choir, and has a reputation for admirable behavior. This is due to the strict discipline maintained by the leader. The congregational singing of the Church is frequently admired by strangers. The choir deserves the credit for whatever excellence has been attained in this direction. The *punctuality* of all its members is as admirable as their reverential demeanor and unselfish devotion to duty. Miss Nellie C. Pettit, Prof. Pettit's daughter, presides at the organ with great ability, while her father conducts the singing. All the music is selected with special reference to its devotional purposes, as it is the theory of the leader and of the Church that Church music is for worship and not for exhibition.

7. TRUSTEES.

The following gentlemen at different times, from 1871 to 1878, served on the Board of Trustees:

A. T. Briggs.
F. R. Chambers.
G. W. Clarke, Ph.D.
F. M. Deems, M.D.
C. R. Disosway.
R. C. Gardner.
*J. Lorimer Graham.**
J. E. Halsey.
W. M. Hutson.
R. H. Johnson.
C. W. Keep.
J. J. Little.
T. E. F. Randolph.
J. R. Reed.

J. Sherwood.
N. W. Smith.
Prof. C. S. Stone.
S. T. Taylor.
H. M. Ware.
Geo. W. Wilson.
W. J. Woodward.
D. B. Clark, M.D.
R. L. Crawford.
J. E. Hoagland.
J. Kleckner.
R. Cottier.
A. P. Crane.
J. W. Downing.

At the Annual Meeting held December 31, 1877, the Board was reorganized, and since that time the following is the list:

Elected.	Retired.	Elected.	Retired.
1877..Joseph J. Little.....	1887	1879..*Charles H. Messer*...	1880
" ..Jer. Sherwood.......	1879	" ..Henry Grasse......	1884
" ..F. A. Crane........	1878	" ..*John Bedford*.......	1883
" ..Robert L. Crawford.		1880..Richard P. Salter...	1883
" ..D. B. Clark, M.D...	1878	1881..Theo. R. Cooke....	
" ..John W. Downing..	1879	1883..Wm. A. McLaughlin	1885
" ..A. P. Crane........	1878	" ..George H. Clayton..	
" ..Robert Cottier	1883	1884..Owen O. Schimmel.	
" ..F. M. Deems, M.D.	1881	" ..Jas. E. Downes....	
1878..Samuel A. Swart....	1885	1885..Wm. D. Swart.....	
" ..Wm. Mitchell......	1879	" ..Geo. W. Olivit.....	
" ..Samuel B. Downes.		1886...Wm. S. Witham...	

* Names of deceased persons printed in italics.

8. ADVISORY COUNCIL.

The following is a complete list of the names of gentlemen who have been members of the Advisory Council:

Appointed.	*Retired.*	*Appointed.*	*Retired.*
1870..Norman W. Smith..	1871	1874..John King..........	1876
" ..Wm. M. Hutson....	1871	1876..George Taylor.......	1884
" ..J. B. Birmingham...	1871	1877..George W. Wilson..	1879
" ..G. W. Clarke, Ph.D.		" ..Wm. H. Conklin....	1885
" .. *J. Sherwood*........	1874	" ..George W. Olivit....	1885
" .. *S. T. Taylor*........	1874	" ..Samuel A. Swart......	1889
" ..Wm. J. Woodward..	1873	1879.. J. H. Fletcher......	1882
1871.., *J. E. Hoagland*.....	1872	" ..W. A. McLaughlin..	1881
" ..T. E. F. Randolph..	1877	1881..John R. Pope......	
" .. *H. W. McDonnell*..	1877	1882..Robert Cottier......	
1872..J. N. Daggett......	1873	1884..Frederic Wheeler...	1886
1873..F. R. Chambers.....	1877	1885..Wm. H. Robertson..	
" ..W. E. Sheldon.....	1877	" ..John Forsyth......	
1874..Jacob R. Reed.		1886..Eli A. Race........	

XVII

Reception of the Pastor on His Return from the East.

ON the 30th of December, 1879, Rev. Dr. Deems, the Pastor of the Church of the Strangers, left the city of New York, in the steamship *Germanic*, to make a tour in the East. This was done at the unanimous recommendation of the officers of the Church, with, it is believed, the cordial indorsement of all the members.

To build up such an institution as the Church of the Strangers, it will readily be perceived, required great care, caution, skill, and labor. From the second Sunday in July, 1866, until now the Sunday service has never been suspended, except twice for repairs. This, together with extraordinary pastoral work devolved on the Doctor by the fact that everything had to be done from the beginning, and by the other fact that the very name of the Church increased the number of those who felt that they had claims upon him, had been a severe tax. The marvel is that his health did not break down under it ; instead, he had been out of his pulpit because of sickness only one Sunday in thirteen years and a half. But, looking to the future, he and the officers of the Church concluded that all parties would receive benefit by a total cessation, for a season, of pastoral anxiety.

It so happened that the Pastor's son, Rev. Edward M. Deems, now Pastor of the Westminster Presbyterian Church in the city of New York, had recently returned from Europe, and, being without a charge, was induced to take the pastorate of the Church during his father's absence. We had known him from his boyhood; he had gone from our Church into the Christian ministry; we could trust him; and so with his father's consent he was called. How faithfully and successfully he discharged his duties is set forth elsewhere. He was ably aided in the pulpit by Rev. Drs. John Hall, Patton, Bevan, Northrop, McArthur, J. H. Vincent, Spenser, and Rev. Messrs. McCowan, Williamson, Rossiter, Ledwith, and Sanders.

Notwithstanding all the success which the Lord granted us in the absence of the Pastor, we felt glad when the time of his return arrived. The Monthly Meeting, which is the governing body of the Church, appointed the following persons as a Committee of Reception:

J. J. Little, R. L. Crawford, Geo. Taylor, Prof. G. W. Pettit, J. H. Fletcher, T. E. F. Randolph, Hon. Geo. W. Clarke, T. H. Cooke; Mrs. F. A. Vanderbilt, Mrs. E. Lonsdale, Mrs. S. K. Hunt, Mrs. W. A. McLaughlin, Mrs. A. E. Pope, Miss C. Sturtevant, Miss M. St. John.

It was ascertained that the *Celtic*, of the White Star line, in which the Pastor was to sail, would leave Liverpool on Thursday, the 17th of June, and would probably reach New York on Sunday, the 27th. Early that morning it was telegraphed that the steamer was approaching. At half-past seven A.M. Dr. Deems was received at the pier by members of the Committee of Reception, accompanied by the Pastor's sons. It was arranged that his congregation should allow him two days of entire rest with his family.

On Tuesday evening, the 29th, a reception was given him. The church and chapel were thrown open. The wall behind the pulpit had been re-painted and ornamented with appropriate inscriptions through the liberality and good taste of Mrs. F. A. Vanderbilt. It had been known that, as he left it, that particular part of the building had been offensive to the Pastor's eyes. To give him a pleasant surprise, he and his family were conducted to the front of the church and first shown this improvement, with which he expressed his entire satisfaction and great delight.

The Committee then escorted the Pastor to the chapel, which was crowded to its utmost capacity. Here he was received with cheers. Over the raised platform in the east of the chapel the ladies had the words " WELCOME HOME " illumined by gas jets. T. E. F. Randolph, Esq., the President of the Monthly Meeting, presided, and opened the proceedings by a few appropriate remarks, and called on Prof. George W. Pettit to lead the congregation in singing "Home, Sweet Home." A very tender prayer, full of thanksgiving, was then offered by George Taylor, Esq., of the Advisory Council.

The Pastor was next welcomed in a speech by the President of the Board of Trustees.

ADDRESS BY JOSEPH J. LITTLE, ESQ.

"*My dear Pastor, Mr. Chairman, Ladies and Gentlemen :*

"We meet together to-night under very pleasant auspices, to greet our Pastor after his long absence, to shake him by the hand, and to feel his friendly clasp in return. We meet to speak to each other words of affection, to renew our mutual pledges of personal friendship, and show our devotion to the Church of the Strangers.

"Indeed, I feel, dear Pastor, that we have occasion for mutual congratulations and joyfulness that so many of us are able to meet you again in health in this place, and, while appreciating the privilege of being permitted to say to you a few words of formal welcome, I regret for your sake that it has not fallen upon a more experienced person, one who could more fully express to you our feelings upon this occasion. While we had no doubt that it would give pleasure to many of your brother ministers to accept an invitation to be present and lend to the occasion their eloquence, we preferred to make it a strictly Church reunion, believing that that would be most agreeable to your own feelings. For my part, I shall trust to your tried friendship to supply what, from lack of experience, I may omit to say, being assured that our feelings of friendship and of brotherly and sisterly affection can be but feebly expressed by anything that may be said by me.

"I well remember that in uttering our farewells to you, one of our brethren said, 'We are glad to see you go.' Although that was spoken in jest, it was no doubtful compliment. We *were* all glad to see you go; not that we desired your absence; not but that many a misgiving arose in our minds as to the dangers attending your long journey; not that we were without apprehension as to the effects of that long absence upon our Church—the Church which is so dear to us all : but we were glad because you felt your future usefulness depended upon a total rest and change of scene, and we were willing to make personal sacrifices rather than endanger that.

" But, sir, if for those reasons we were glad to see you go, we are now doubly glad to welcome you back, and to receive from you the assurances that the trip has not been in vain ; that the object sought has been attained ; that you feel renewed in strength and better fitted for the work before you. It gives me great pleasure to assure you of the love and unity that have existed among us during your absence. This absence fully demonstrates to our minds that the existence of the Church of the Strangers as an unsectarian Christian Church is no longer an experiment. Notwithstanding the doubts and fears of many as to the possibility of establishing and maintaining such a Church, to be supported as a free Church, and especially in this section of the city, it was established, and with you here it was maintained for twelve years, and now, sir, its members have maintained it for six months in your absence.

" When you shook our hands upon your departure, you left us united in fraternal love and free from the burden of debt. We now, sir, again submit the Church to your care, united in the same bonds of love, and also free from the burden of debt. During all your absence no meetings of the Church, of the Sunday School, or of any of the boards of officers have been omitted. Every Sunday service has been regularly held. No Communion service has passed without adding members to our numbers. Our finances have not been kept up by special collections in the Church, nor by solicitations of money outside; but upon your departure the Board of Finance, in a circular letter, addressed only to the members of the Church, stated what, in their judgment, would be necessary to make up for our increased expenses, and probable decreased Sunday collections; and the only strife that has existed in our midst during the past six months has been a fraternal strife of members to bear each his proper, full, and equitable portion of the burden. The result has been that all obligations have been regularly and promptly discharged, and the Church treasury has never been entirely empty.

" Although, sir, we do not wish to cast a shadow upon this pleasant reunion, this short account of the Church would not be complete should I omit to say that *death* has entered our midst, to remind us of the frailty of human life. Hands that once you clasped you will clasp no more on earth; but we have the blessed consolation of believing that those who have been called away from earth's busy scenes, went in the full hope of the glory of the resurrection.

" Neither are we unmindful that there are other ties

now to be broken, ties that have been formed with him you left with us as Pastor while you were away. But of that another is to speak, and, as I know all are anxious to hear your voice, I will now, on behalf of every one present, as well as those who are necessarily absent, but whose hearts we know are here, salute you in the words which the ladies of the Committee have so beautifully illumined, 'Welcome Home.' May you be spared for many years of usefulness in the vineyard of the Master, and may the love now existing between you and your flock never perish, either in this world or beyond the grave—is not only the prayer of him who now speaks to you, but also the universal wish of the Church.

"It gives me very great pleasure to present to you, on behalf of many of your friends, whose names are inclosed, this testimonial as a token of their fraternal love. [Here he presented the Pastor a purse containing a handsome sum of money.] It is not given so much on account of its intrinsic worth or pecuniary value, as to more fully indicate that at this time we renew our pledges of personal friendship, and our devotion to the cause represented by this Church.

REPLY BY REV. DR. DEEMS.

"*Mr. Chairman, my dear Brother Little, Sisters and Brethren :*

"I am taken at a delightful disadvantage by this display of kindness on the part of the officers and members of our beloved Church. No hint had been given me that I should be expected to say or do anything to-night beyond grasping again the warm hands which dropped from mine on that cold December night when we parted.

"There has been a little mysteriousness about movements since my arrival. Our steamer reached the pier at seven o'clock last Sunday morning, and I was met by a Committee of Church officers, who conducted me to my home. A thorough rest of ten days, during an exceptionally tranquil voyage, had set me up, and I told them that I should be at Church. They exchanged glances of distress, and undertook to tell me that I was too tired! and to advise me to remain with my family!! Of course, I expected to 'remain with my family'; but couldn't I just as well remain with them in Church? The friendly officers did not take into account the rare pleasure it is for a Pastor to sit in a pew, in a pew beside his wife; nor did they seem to think that naturally, as a Christian, I longed to hear the Gospel, and, as a Pastor, longed to see my own church sanctuary. But you know what an obedient Pastor I have always been! and so I succumbed! This evening I learned what it meant. When you met me at the church door, and under the lights there was displayed to me the newly and beautifully ornamented apse, with the appropriate inscription and decorations with which it was adorned, I saw that you were kindly keeping this as a surprise, to increase the delights which you are heaping upon my reception.

"And now, in this crowded chapel, you have spoken,

by the lips of the President of your Board of Trustees, such manly, kind, and Christian words of greeting as go to my very heart, and awaken a most cordial response of reciprocation.

"As to the long tour which I have accomplished, I shall have other occasions on which to address you. But one thing you will be glad to know, and that is, that I have spent six months of total freedom from the cares which for over thirteen years have pressed upon my spirit. It is my good fortune to have the happy faculty of being altogether in the place where I am ; so, when I went away, I left entirely. For my Church, for my family, for all with whom I was connected, I made the most complete arrangements within my power. I knew the officers of the Church. I knew you. I knew my son, whom you had called to be your temporary Pastor. I knew the Great Head of the Church. I knew that I could do nothing more for you before my return, and that if I suffered myself to be fretted by solicitude, the whole intent of my separation from all I most loved would be defeated.

"My friends, if I had gone pleasure-seeking, if I had become tired of my work and disgusted with the Christian ministry, if I had fled, like Jonah, from some divinely imposed but disagreeable mission, I could not have had this freedom from care. But knowing in the depths of my heart, that my tour was undertaken in the interests of this Church, and for the increase of the usefulness of my future ministry, I had no misgivings and no anxiety. Does not this

Church belong to the Lord? Do not I belong to the Lord? Will He not care for His own as much when we are separated as when we are together? I had served the Church thirteen years. The first eight years and five months were without a Sunday of vacation. A few weeks, two or three times, in the latter years had been spent out of the city. Such continuance in labor in the same sphere, such frequency of preaching in the same pulpit, summer and winter, was calculated to beget sameness and dullness and running in ruts. It seemed to me necessary for my mental health that I should have a total change of scene. So I went into a desert place apart.

" If the first motion to go was personal, I should have been exceedingly obtuse not to have soon seen that our Lord had designs concerning *you* and the Church of the Strangers in this temporary separation. Our history is peculiar. Your Pastor was not ' called,' as his brethren have been, to the pastorate of an organized Church. You have gathered around me, and the providence of God has raised you up an independent Christian body, an ecclesiasticized Evangelical Alliance, to represent the charities and unities of Protestant Christianity. From time to time it has been predicted that the experiment would be a failure. We are far down town. *There is no other church building in this city in so obscure a place as this.* No street cars nor omnibuses pass in front of us. We are on the last block of a street which is not long and is occupied by business houses. We are not even on a corner. Such is now the position of our beautiful church, which, when it was erected, was the cathedral of Presbyterianism in America. You must come in front of it to see it.

" Now, whether such an organized Christian society as ours, unconnected with any of the sects, could sustain itself down town is a question which has exercised many persons. For myself, it does not seem a matter of paramount importance. If the Lord has no need of this Church, I am sure that I have not ; if He has, He will take care of His own. But very often it was not only insinuated but asserted that this Church was kept alive by the exertions of the Pastor, and sometimes that has been put forth as a compliment to me. We have tested that question. I have not written you a line of direction or advice about the economies of the Church during my absence, and under God you have carried the Church along quite as well as I have ever been able to do. So, in the future, I shall be relieved of any anxiety on that sub-·ject, and also from similar prophecies.

" If I have had no anxiety about the Church, dear friends, I have not suspended my affection for you. My eyes have been running over this crowded chapel to-night, and their report is that there are no faces present, except those of strangers, which I have not seen with the eyes of my heart, while riding Egyptian donkeys, Arabian camels, or Syrian horses—faces that have risen up before me as I have gazed on the skies which hang over the lands made holy by the residence of prophets and apostles and of the Son of God. Now, my happiness is to see those faces once more 'in the flesh.'

" I have no promises to make. I have formed no new resolutions. But I trust that all that I have seen in distant lands, and all my experiences may come out in my future ministry, so as to be profitable to us all. My heart is filled with delight at your unity and co-operation, your faith and zeal, your hope and charity. Some have left us and gone up to other mansions of the Father's house. You will follow them. When the hour of your departure comes, may you find on that other shore, as I found on landing, friends to cluster lovingly about you, and amid the illumination of the Upper Temple see glowing with the light of love for *you* the words which you have emblazoned above my head, ' Welcome Home.'

" Mr. Chairman, my dear brother who has addressed me, dear brothers and sisters all, I thank you from my heart of hearts for your warm and generous acts and words. You know how I feel better than I can tell you."

The chairman then called upon Dr. Clarke to express the sentiments of the Church toward the temporary Pastor.

ADDRESS BY HON. GEORGE W. CLARKE TO REV. ED-WARD M. DEEMS.

" *Respected Sir :* I am instructed by the Reception Committee to make to you on this occasion a presentation of the regards of the Church of the Strangers.

"I need not tell you that this is a very agreeable duty for me to perform toward one who has been to me both *pupil** and *Pastor*. I watched with deep interest your progress through college and the theological seminary, as I have also the labors of your ministry; and *now* I have the honor of tendering you the greetings of the good people of this Church, who have for six months enjoyed your pastoral care.

"I am aware that the offer of this service to you by our unanimous choice was a surprise, both to yourself and your beloved father. But, to the delight of us all, it was finally accepted, and you entered on this half year's ministry in a spirit of Christian manhood that won all our hearts; telling us frankly in the outset that you assumed the work of your father in his absence at our earnest request, not for the purpose of holding together the congregation of the Church of the Strangers, but, by the blessing of God, with the view of building up His people and saving souls.

"It was a great responsibility—and, no doubt, you said to yourself, as young Solomon did when called to take the place of *his* father, 'I am but a little child, I know not how to go out or come in. Give thy servant therefore, O Lord, an understanding heart, that he may discern the path of duty toward this Thy people.' As in the case of the young king God gave him more than he asked, so in *yours* He has enabled

---

* Dr. Clarke was for years the Principal of Mt. Washington Collegiate Institute, in which Rev. Edward M. Deems had been a pupil.

you to care for His people here, and keep the congregation together besides.

"We can, therefore, assure you in all truthfulness that you have not hid your talents in a napkin, but are able to return them unto your Lord with usury.

"Henceforth, reverend and dear sir, your relations to your father will be greatly enlarged—you will still be his son, but you will also be his Christian brother and friend in the ministry of the Word.*

"Saved from the perils of sea and land, *he* comes back with renewed strength, as we hope, to minister again to the people of his love, and *you* go to your already chosen field. The Lord go with you, as will also the prayers of this people.

"And now, in the name of the officers and members of the Church of the Strangers and its congregation, I present you this testimonial of their good will, with the qualifying remark, that whatever may be its pecuniary value, it must not be regarded by you as representing the full measure of esteem and affection in which you are held by us all."

This address was accompanied by a purse of money.

REV. EDWARD M. DEEMS'S RESPONSE.

"*Mr. President, and Friends of the Church of the Strangers :*

"In calling upon me to make the last address on this delightful occasion, I perceive that your Committee have done exactly what I feared they would;

---

* Alluding to the fact that the Rev. E. M. Deems had become Pastor of the Westminster Church in New York.

they have first served you generously with ice-cream and strawberries and other delicious viands, and then made the exacting demand of you that you should finish your repast with roast beef and potatoes, the very commonest substantials. The only way of escape open to me is through brevity.

" The period of six months which I have just spent as temporary Pastor of the Church of the Strangers marks an epoch in my life. It has been a season of happiness for me, not only because I have formed so many delightful friendships among this people, but also because I have been conscious of having tried to serve my Master with a zeal and energy surpassing anything of the kind in the past of my career. The earth gives to the sky her moisture, only to find it quickly coming back to her to reward her with the grateful showers which cause her grass, and grain, and flowers to spring up and bud, and blossom, and bloom. Just so the labors which I have given to God for you in the past six months, have returned upon my head rich with blessings from above.

" I do most humbly trust that this night finds me not only a happier but also a stronger man in every way than I was six months ago, when I tremblingly took upon me the temporary pastorate of your Church. So it has been a *profitable* season with me. In conducting the executive part of the work of the Pastor of such a Church as this, and in giving to a people who deserved and could appreciate it the best that my mental storehouse could furnish, I have had an intellectual discipline which must prove a help to me throughout all my future ministry. But I thank God that the profits which I have derived from my labors in this Church have not been merely intellectual. I have, I trust, grown in grace and become a better man for all my labors for and with you. The communion which I have had with you in the home-circle, in the Prayer Meeting, and in the house of the Lord, has been so true and so sweet that to-night I feel nearer to God than I have ever been before.

" You have already had your attention directed to the fact that the Church of the Strangers has most successfully stood the strain which the Pastor's six months' absence has put upon it. Who is to have the honor of this success? *The Lord God, our Heavenly Father.* Had He withdrawn His presence from us, we should have soon been wrecked. But He did not do so. The Lord of Hosts has been with us, and as to-night we contemplate with satisfaction the happy condition of this Church upon the return of its Pastor, let us all unite in saying from our hearts, Let glory be given ' not unto us, O Lord! not unto us, but unto Thy name !' "

" And yet I feel that I ought to add that while, *primarily*, the successful conduct of the affairs of the Church of the Strangers during the Pastor's absence has been due to the presence and blessing of God, *the instrumentality used has been the people of the Church.* In the days of Nehemiah it was because ' *the people* had a mind to work ' that the wall of the city of the great king was built up successfully. So the fact that the Pastor returns to find the Church in so good a condition, is due to the fact that the people have each and all wrought faithfully, and as in the sight of the Great Head of the Church.

"And now let me give to the Church of the Strangers a slight expression of gratitude, which is too deep to be fully told to you. You have stood by me to a man; officers, choir, Sunday School, members of the Church, and members of the congregation. You might have kept me for six months on a mental rack, and broken my heart by needlessly laying upon me burdens which you have borne in silence, by coldness in spiritual things, or by neglect in attending upon the services of the sanctuary, or by dissension among yourselves, or by some such thing; but so far from doing this, you have prayed for me and labored for and with me. I thank you. May God richly reward you for all your goodness to me.

" Dr. Clarke, you spoke truly when you said in your address, that I should henceforth stand in a new relation to my father. I certainly shall. I shall sympathize with him as never in the past. I thought before he left us that I appreciated in a great measure the trying nature of his position as Pastor of this Church. But I have discovered that I have had but a faint conception of the burden which he has been bearing for these long years. From the name and nature of this Church its Pastor comes to have probably the most trying parish in our land, and perhaps in any land. I need not undertake to tell you how this comes about. But take my word for it, if there is a man in this world who needs your prayers, your sympathy, your help, your charity and consideration, it is this man, my good father, your faithful Pastor. Sustain and cheer him in every possible way, and may he and you, as Pastor and people, long continue to be in the future what you have been in the past, a benediction to this great city, to this great country, and to humanity! Farewell."

At the conclusion of the speeches, the Pastor was conducted to the church parlor, which had been tastefully decorated by the ladies, and all present had an opportunity of greeting him personally. After refreshments had been served, the remainder of the evening was spent in social enjoyment.

On the following Sunday the Church was beautifully ornamented with flowers, and there was one of the largest gatherings for the Holy Communion ever assembled in that building.

XVIII.

"How" and "Why."

MUCH of what is written in the preceding pages might be called a history of the structure—*anatomy*—of the Church of the Strangers. Of equal importance is the question of function—the *physiology* of the organization. In the hope of illustrating this by looking through the eyes and thinking and feeling through the brains and hearts of others, the Editor addressed to various members of the Church the following formula:

" Please write out an account of *how* and *why* you came to join the Church of the Strangers. Make it as long or as short as you please, and write in a familiar style. No names will be published."

The replies found below fully justify every expectation entertained of them. They convey an idea of the Church's influence by describing the effect of that influence upon those who were swayed by it. It is a method of studying cause by investigating effect. As these are but fair samples, selected at random, they constitute, let us hope, the Church's sufficient *raison d'etre.*—J. S. T.

FROM A JEWELER.

" I was brought up in the Church of England, but before reaching manhood, had turned my back upon religion. First in London and afterwards in the country, I led a life far removed from the teachings of Christianity. That I did not plunge into ruin deeper even than I did, is due, I firmly believe, to the restraining hand of God.

" After I married I led a 'moral' life, because my love of wife and home made it easy to do so. My early training now prompted me to go to Church on Sundays; and happening into the Church of the Strangers, I was impressed by the simple, earnest preaching I heard there, and soon became a pretty regular attendant. Sometimes, upon hearing the preacher speak of the love of Jesus and the necessity of accepting His salvation, I would almost resolve to do it, but always put it off again, and the impression passed away. But yet conviction deepened. I am not impressionable. I know some are converted instantaneously; *others it takes years.* I was of the latter class.   .

" At last my little baby girl became ill; it turned out to be diphtheria—and baby died. Now, a parent will understand how I loved my little one. And as she lay there in her childish beauty, I began to ask, ' Shall I see her again?'

" At length I resolved to accept the mercy of God through Jesus Christ. I cannot tell the precise moment when I was converted, but I felt sure of salvation by faith in Jesus. I turned away from my old ways and companions, began to go to Prayer Meeting, and every night with my wife read the Scriptures and prayed.

" Still I shrank from joining the Church ; thought I could be as good a Christian out of the Church as in it. About one year after my baby had died I became ill with a serious attack of laryngitis, which it was thought at one time would prove fatal. One day I was in a sort of trance. I seemed to be gone to heaven, and as I entered there I was asked the question : 'To which division of the Lord's army did you belong?'

" I could not answer. I had joined no Church. But I resolved, if the Lord would spare my life, to join the Church of the Strangers at the earliest possible opportunity, on confession. This I did. And although I fear I am but a poor specimen of a Christian, I have never regretted the step.

" I may add that I liked the Church of the Strangers—

" 1. On account of its simple service ;

. " 2. Because Dr. Deems preached Jesus Christ without an 'ism';

" 3. Because I loved the singing of the orphan children."

FROM A PROFESSIONAL MAN.

" I united with the Church on account of its broad Christian principles, and the welcome to strangers which it originated."

FROM A YOUNG MAN IN BUSINESS.

" In 1881 Dr. Deems preached a sermon on the following text, taken from Gen. xxxix. 9 : *How then can I do this great wickedness, and sin against God ?* My mother heard the sermon and repeated it to me when she came home from Church. I did not pay much attention to it then, as I was not a Christian. But one night, about five months later, the words came to me with such power, I could no longer resist giving my heart to God. And as Dr. Deems and my mother had sowed the seed that thus took root, I of course joined the Church of which they were members. This answers the *How* of your inquiry.

" I united with the Church to promote the glory of Christ, and to advance His kingdom. I believe it is the Christian's duty to belong to some branch of the Christian Church. This is the *Why.*"

FROM A WIDOW.

" I was brought up, I might almost say, in the Madison Square Presbyterian Church, which was formerly the old Broome Street Church. Rev. Dr. Adams had been my Pastor from as far back as I can remember. When he died the pew rents in my Church had become so high that I could not afford longer to hold two sittings, so I began to look around among other Churches, to see if I could be suited as to the preaching and the pew rents. It fell in my way to visit the Church of the Strangers, which I did one Sunday morning. But the Church was so crowded that I was obliged to sit on a camp stool in one of the aisles. Whether from my uncomfortable surroundings, or a spell of fidgets, I went away with the impression that I should not care to go back.

" Some time after, a lady of the Church suggested to me that a second visit might make a different impression upon me. I yielded to her wishes, and went once more to hear Dr. Deems. This time I had a good seat in the body of the Church—and cried all through the sermon ! The case was soon decided. I joined the Church of the Strangers.

" I do not suppose that any child was ever more strictly brought up than I was. The welts on my back rise up yet and accuse the mistaken piety that inflicted them ! In our house the rod was part of the mantel furniture. Every day of my life I was obliged to read two chapters out of the Old Testament, and one out of the New. That took me through in a year. When it came dinner time I would hear, ' Well, Miss, have you read your chapters ? ' If I had not finished them, I could have no dinner. In this way I began to dislike the Bible, and with all my reading I got no instruction.

" Dr. Deems undid this early error. It is he that has taught me to pray, to read the Bible, to love my fellow-creatures. I never open the Bible now but I see something new."

FROM A YOUNG SCOTCHMAN.

" My principal reason for joining the Church of the Strangers, was the fact that it is undenominational.

I attended some time before I became a member. Conviction told me that inside, not outside, of the Church was the proper place for me."

FROM A YOUNG MAN.

"Replying to the question as to why I came to the Church of the Strangers, I have only to say that I went first to the Church on the recommendation of a friend who wished me to hear Dr. Deems preach. I was not then a member of any Church, but from a sermon I heard I was convinced of my duty to join some Christian body ; and in making a selection, if one thing more than another influenced me, outside of the personality of the Pastor, which I think is always one of the first considerations, it was the un-sectarian principle on which the Church is founded."

FROM THE FATHER OF THE ABOVE.

"In answer to your inquiry as to *how* and *why* I came to join the Church of the Strangers, I offer the following reasons:

" 1. I liked the preaching ;
" 2. It was convenient to my house ;
" 3. It is unsectarian ;
" 4. It is not rich and fashionable."

FROM A WIDOW.

"It was the *home feeling* which pervades our Church that first attracted me. I came from a dear New England Church, to which from childhood I had been devoted. At last I found myself a stranger in

this vast metropolis, wandering for a year in search of
a spiritual Home.   By accident (if such there be in
our guided lives) I came into a Friday-night Prayer
Meeting conducted by the Pastor of this Church.
The search was ended and the choice made.   And
when, on a Monday evening soon after, myself and
daughter presented ourselves as candidates for admission to the Church of the Strangers, and Dr. Deems
said to me, 'And what led you and your daughter to
come to us?' I could truly say: 'The fact, sir, that
we have found a Home!'"

FROM A TRUSTEE.

"Some fifteen years ago my wife and I, then unac-
quainted in the city, started out from West Third
Street to find the residence of a Lutheran minister
who lived in East Seventh Street.   Supposing that
all streets in that part crossed the city in straight
lines, we counted from West Third and concluded
Clinton Place must be Seventh Street.   Accordingly
we started on that thoroughfare to find the house of
the Lutheran Pastor.   When we had crossed Fifth
Avenue, we found a crowd of people on the sidewalk
going in the same direction we were going; and when
they got to Mercer Street they all turned to the right.
We concluded to follow this crowd.   We were led
into a Church; opening one of the hymn-books which
I found in the pew, I discovered that we were in the
'Church of the Strangers.'   I said at once, 'Why,
this is the Church for us: *we* are strangers.'

"We never found the Lutheran Minister.   I have

been a regular attendant of the Church from that day to this."

FROM A BUSINESS MAN.

"Some time in 1867 or '68 I first heard Dr. Deems preach in the Hedding M. E. Church, East 17th St. I was so much pleased with him that I determined to attend whatever Church he might be called to in this city.

"A few months after my marriage (May, 1870) I learned from the newspapers that he had located in our present quarters, and I have been attending ever since."

FROM AN ARTIST.

"I was taught in early childhood to believe in God and His only begotten Son our Redeemer; but I did not join any Church for many years. I came to New York in 1870. Coming down University Place one Sunday morning, my attention was attracted by a placard reading, 'Church of the Strangers,' at the entrance to the University building. That appeal made me think. I was a 'stranger;' and I concluded this must be *my* Church. I stepped inside and heard Dr. Deems for the first time. I have not yet recovered from the powerful effects of that sermon."

FROM A PUBLISHER.

"My father was an English clergyman; one of the best and most amiable of men. I should have had every advantage in youth, if I had not come under the pernicious influence of my step-mother. She was a 'professed' Christian and a talented woman, but possessed the kind of character to impress a youth with the idea that there is such a thing as hypocrisy in the world, and at any rate, that not all 'Christians' are lovable beings. I kept pretty straight, and saw little of any kind of vice before my twenty-second year. I then met *with the great disappointment of my life;* but, after a few weeks of melancholy, determined to throw off all that, and as I could not have the *best thing in life,* to have what I foolishly thought the next best. And having at that time excellent health, I entered into all kinds of gayety and self-gratification with avidity. I cannot say I was really happy ; but yet I cannot understand how I enjoyed life as much as I did, while I saw I was grieving my best friends and had deliberately turned my back upon the God I had been taught to love as well as reverence. *I never could be a hypocrite.* This, with perhaps the fact that I always shrank from leading others, male or female, from the path of virtue, is all I can say in my own favor. Rather wishing to escape from friends whom I was only distressing, I came to this country and lived for some years a most reckless life, seeking only to gratify the senses, without any regard for the future in this life or the next.

   " During this time I was always making a good living; in fact, was respected in business, though known to be living a fast life. At my father's death I received a few thousand dollars. It was the loss of this—and other troubles—that seemed to lead me—like another prodigal—to come to myself. I commenced attending Church pretty regularly and joined the Y. M. C. A. I *knew* all the truths of the Gospel by heart, and the most brilliant sermon had no effect unless I felt sure the preacher himself was genuinely in earnest. From what source I hardly know, I got the conviction that Dr. Deems was a truly good and earnest man. I went to hear him, and a sermon of his on the Fifty-first Psalm, in which he brought out very forcibly David's desire for *purity* as well as *pardon,*—was really the deciding point in my life. I did not wait long before I joined the Church ; and I am sure that being actively engaged in various fields of usefulness has helped me to remain faithful. I shall always feel for Dr. Deems the respect and affection of a son."

FROM A PROFESSIONAL GENTLEMAN.

"You ask me to tell you 'how' and 'why' I came to join the Church of the Strangers; and I shall answer your question without reservation.

"As you know, I was born and brought up in a foreign country and in a Church, which, *for me*, had no Gospel, no God, no Saviour, no infallibility ; but superstitions, and fallibilities, and formulas in abundance.

"When I came to this blessed country eighteen years ago, and in the thirtieth of my life, I heard for the first time the preaching of the Gospel. There was an expansion of ideas so novel to me that I was struck with wonder. I had never read the Bible, because that is forbidden literature in the Church from which I came. From motives of curiosity, I procured a Bible, and not merely *read,* but *devoured* the sacred words, especially of the New Testament. I came to the conclusion that I had been living for thirty years in complete ignorance of who I was, whence I had come, and whither I was going. I realized that the worldly pleasures in which I had indulged so many years were but carnal sins which gradually transform a man into a mere animal with only material desires and passions, and without a single spark of spiritual life.

" I candidly confess, my dear friend, that no logic or rhetoric can convey to a man's mind an idea of the remorse, the suffering, the humiliation and degradation I felt when I learned what a sinner I was.

" What did I do then ?—Well, for the first time in my life, I *prayed*—prayed in earnest, with my whole heart and soul, not for forgiveness merely, but for a change of heart, and spiritual light. I desired acceptance in the eyes of my Saviour rather than of my fellow-men.

" But you may be impatient to know what all this has to do with your ' *how* ' and ' *why.*'

" Let us see. The preceding events led to a determination on my part to join some Church, where the inspired words are explained. Choice number one was a colossal blunder ; for my poor heart was hungering for the living bread, and they handed me a basket filled with *flowers and adorning ribbons!* In other words, the discourses of the Pastor were beautiful pieces of oratory, but very indifferent explanations of

Holy Scripture. I can assure you that I was spiritually hungry indeed, and remained so. I found that
by reading the Bible I could obtain more light than
by listening to such discourses. I determined, therefore, to hear other Pastors, and again fell into a trap.
Oh! my friend, my friend, the Lord deliver you from
a fashionable Church! I can assure you that my experience in the two Churches mentioned almost
turned me into an atheist, a heathen, an—I know
not what! One thing is certain,—I became skeptical;
I no longer believed in anything. All was worldli-
ness; even the inspired words appeared simply lectures in a school of morality, written and conceived
by man alone. The richness of the surroundings, the
profuse display of worldly wealth, the hiring of the
pews, in a house dedicated to the worship of God,
the magnificent pieces of oratory, the sectarianism,
the churchism—all these appeared to my mind again
like the mummery of the Church in which I was
brought up. I suffered a spiritual relapse which was
more serious than the original disease!

"But the Master who orders all things opened, in
His providence, a new source of light. At this time
my dear wife insisted on my going to hear Dr. Deems
preach. I went, and with a slight variation ot
Cæsar's phrase, I was obliged to say, *I came, I saw,
and was conquered!* I found in Dr. Deems an earnestness in expounding the Gospel which I had never
heard before; and the more I heard him, the more I
regained my faith. The horizon of the dark and tur-
bulent sea on which I was drifting ready to give up

hope, became clear and bright. The inner man underwent a metamorphosis. I began to feel that some sincerity, after all, remained in this world. I found in the discourses all the logic and rhetoric I wanted, sufficient clearness to enable me to know what the Master wants me to do, and above all, an earnestness which convinced me that the preacher was intent on saving my soul.

"Now, what about the Church of the Strangers? Is it perfect, in my humble opinion?

"I will frankly answer, No; it is defective, as all human institutions are. But the simplicity of its management and its services was just the antidote for that formality which had so nearly made me an atheist. I must confess, too, that as yet, I am but a babe in Christ; I go to Church chiefly for what I can get, for the preaching of its Pastor. The organization and departments of the Church are therefore of secondary importance to me. I am convinced that there is no Christianity in *mere* Church work; in fact, I believe that the practical, technical part of it would divert my mind from the spirituality which I so much need and which had been so thoroughly crushed out of me by a Church which was nothing *but* formality and technicality.

"If there be sentiments in the above which seem uncharitable, you must remember the circumstances of the writer, who simply gives *his* experience."

THE VANDERBILT MEMORIAL TABLET.

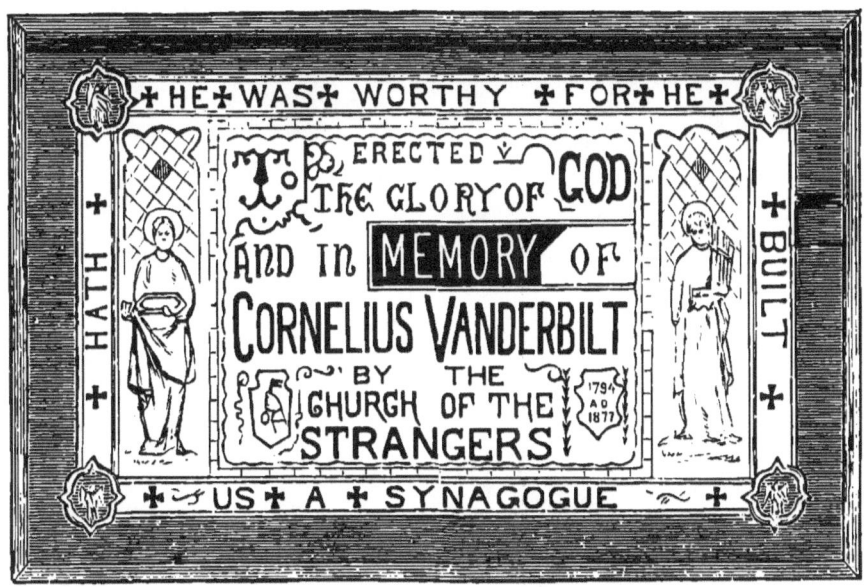

THE ABOVE REPRESENTS A BEAUTIFULLY WROUGHT BRONZE TABLET TO THE ME-
MORY OF CORNELIUS VANDERBILT, WHICH WAS UNVEILED ON THE AFTERNOON OF
DECEMBER 6, 1879, IN THE CHURCH OF THE STRANGERS, TO SHOW THE ESTEEM IN
WHICH THE CHURCH HOLDS HIS MEMORY.   IT IS PLACED IN THE NORTH WALL OF
THE CHURCH TO THE LEFT AS SEEN BY THE CONGREGATION.

FROM A YOUNG WOMAN.

" I was an utter stranger in New York, and was employed as a governess. There was neither friend nor companion to whom I might go for sympathy or comfort. One evening, in a fit of anger, I rushed out of the house, determined never to return to it.

." I walked for a little while in Washington Square, until I became calm enough to reflect on the conséquences of my rash act. I examined my purse, and found that it contained about fifty cents. By degrees the seriousness of my situation dawned upon me. But it had not occurred to me that it was too late an hour for a young woman to be in a public park without an escort. I was entirely unconscious of my surroundings until a man approached me with insulting remarks. I turned and ran up Waverley Place, the man pursuing. At Greene Street I turned the corner without knowing where I was. Seeing a light about the middle of the block on the opposite side, I crossed over, rushed in at the open door, up a flight of stairs at the left, and sank exhausted at the top. Here I sat in a dazed condition for a few minutes, when I heard singing in the distance.

" ' Jesus, lover of my soul, '

were the words they sang. I thought of my dear old mother, who used to sing that hymn to me when I was a child. I got up and walked down-stairs in the direction of the singing. It was in an adjoining room. I opened a door and timidly entered. I found a small company of people in a large and cheerful place. An elderly man sat at the piano. When he saw me he arose, came to me, and politely asked me to have a seat. In the course of conversation he asked me whether I had acquaintances present, and I said, 'No.' Then I explained my desperate strait. He encouraged me, and said he would be my friend. He gave me a book and asked me to sing, which I did. Everything was done in a quiet, reverent way. It seemed a devotional meeting, but it was informal.*

*   *   *   *   *   *   *

"The place I had taken refuge in was the chapel of the Church of the Strangers. The singing I heard was a choir rehearsal, and the man who befriended me before asking any questions was Prof. G. W. Pettit, the leader of the choir, and organist in the Church. He said he would introduce me to his Pastor; and by his gentle and Christian conduct and conversation he so wrought upon me that I returned the same night to my situation.

"Soon after I began to attend preaching services in the Church of the Strangers. I knew the Pastor by sight, but still had not been introduced to him.

"One day I was in great trouble, having just received word that my sister—the only support besides myself of my poor old widowed mother in distant Ireland—was dangerously ill. I went out into Washington Square. As I sat there I saw Dr. Deems passing. Instinctively feeling that from him would come sympathy and help, I rose and met him, saying,

---

* See Chap. xvi. for a further history of the Choir.

'Doctor, I have a sister who is dying ; will you pray for her?'

"His reply was, 'God bless you, my daughter, I will. Let us pray for her now.' And raising his hat he then breathed a silent prayer for my sister. Afterwards I announced my name, and explained the circumstances of the case.

"And this is 'how' I came to the Church of the Strangers. In answer to the question 'why' I joined, I can only say, because

"'I was a stranger, and ye took me in.'"

FROM A FORMER MEMBER OF THE ADVISORY COUNCIL.

"You ask me 'How and Why' I came to join the Church of the Strangers. I would gladly answer, but I fear I shall not have time to answer as briefly as you might desire ; and if you have more time than I have, you may trim it down to suit.

"With the contrariness of my people,* I will answer the last part of your question first. 'Why?' Well, on the last night of the year 1870, I was taking stock spiritually. A calm and deliberate examination revealed the fact that I was utterly bankrupt. The balance sheets of former years filed away in my memory showed some small stock of spirituality, and I had been proud of the possession. This time I had none ; and the want of it did not much disturb me. In former years I had times of anxiety, sleepless nights, and

---

* He is a Scotchman.

melancholy days of wrestling with the great problem of life. I was in middle life now, and all such
anxieties had left me. Instead of the yearning desire
for a higher life, I had now a settled code of morality
sufficient to keep up a reputation for honesty—a
Golden Rule which ignored Him who gave it! But
I had one tender spot in my heart, and that spot God
touched. I had motherless children from whom I
had been separated for years. I longed to see them;
and yet I dared not, lest it should be revealed to
them that they had a Godless father.

"No; I would rather die than add such bitterness
to their cup of sorrow. The resolve came upon me
with the weight of a settled conviction, that they
should never see me except as a Christian; and then,
for the first time in years, I prayed—a cold, passion-
less prayer—and while I prayed the thought came to
me, 'Can it be that the Holy Spirit has left me? I
have no feeling now such as I had in days gone by.'
The one definite petition of my prayer was, 'Lord,
let me not see the close of another year except as a
Christian!' I went to bed and slept, and when I
arose on the morning of the New Year I again prayed
that I might not see its close except as a Christian.
I then thought it my duty to *put myself in the way of
becoming* a Christian. · I knew of no Christian Church.
Many, I thought, were anti-Christian—and one I
knew by experience had acted as such. I thought—
and the thought has not quite left me yet—that some
so-called Churches are only social clubs. I looked in
the newspapers, and my weakness was accommodated

by this announcement: 'Church of the Strangers;
strangers welcome ; all seats free.' Now, I had been
a stranger in New York over ten years, and, so far as
the invitation went, that was the Church for me.

" And now comes the answer as to 'How ' I joined
the Church. I went there on the first Sunday in
January, 1871. There was nothing there that I
I could *find fault with !* The rich and the poor were
treated alike. The preacher had wit without flippancy,
and boldness and originality without irreverence.
He hurt my pride a little, but I forgave him ; for I
knew it was only a random shot, and he could not
possibly know me. I was attracted. I went every
Sunday. I stole in late and left early, lest some one
might speak to me, and I might say something to
commit myself. Thus I continued to attend until, one
Sunday in May, one of the ushers, a young man
named Smith, since dead, modestly invited me to
come to the Prayer Meeting. I accepted the invitation, and soon began to be interested; and the interest grew into anxiety—but still I had no prospect of
becoming a Christian. On Communion Sundays I retired to the gallery and looked on, and listened to
what seemed to be my death warrant ; for I had a
belief that God would keep His part of the contract.
The year was half gone when, one day in June,
while sitting in the gallery, the words came to me
that changed the whole course of my life. I know
not what the text was, nor even the subject of the
sermon. I was seized by one sentence, and I heard
no more that day. It was this : 'God says, " My

son, give Me thine heart." The trouble with you is,
you may have offered your time, your money, your
intellect ; you have offered God everything but your
heart. Give God your heart, and all will be well.'
That shot was for me, and it hit the mark. It
troubled me night and day. It humbled me. I had
thought myself a philosopher. I saw that I had
wrestled like a fool. I had boasted :

"' I shall never follow blindly where my Reason cannot go ;
    I shall know by Reason only all that mortals need to know.'

I had learned long before that Love can lead Reason ;
and when the order is reversed it is a very weak love.
I saw that I had never offered God my heart. I resolved to do it now. Overwhelmed with a sense of
my unworthiness and unfitness, I reluctantly went to
see Dr. Deems. I had never spoken to him, and by
way of introduction I sent him a letter, and afterwards called upon him. I expected to have my sin-
ful heart cauterized with theological caustic, and had
braced myself up for the operation ; but instead of
pain he gave me pleasure ; instead of humiliation he
gave me sympathy—' the oil of joy for mourning, the
garment of praise for the spirit of heaviness.'

"With faith small as a grain of mustard seed, I was
admitted to the Church on the first Sunday in July,
1871. I have since celebrated its anniversary as the
day in which I was born into the Kingdom. Surely
no one with a weaker faith ever came to God. And
God hath not despised my poor weak faith, but hath
nourished and strengthened it.

"'Thus far the Lord hath led me on, and in His strength I glory.'"

FROM AN ANDOVER THEOLOGICAL STUDENT.

" How I became acquainted with the Church of the Strangers."

" In the year 1878 I left my home, Antioch, in Syria, Turkey, and went to a village near Antioch for the purpose of teaching and preaching. This town is a few miles north of Seleucia, where Paul and Barnabas embarked for the first time to preach the Gospel to the Gentiles (Acts xiii. 4).

" During my stay in the village, one day a friend of mine, a missionary lady (Mrs. Shattuck), handed me a pamphlet entitled, ' Metropolitan Pulpit,' which contained sermons and sketches of some eminent preachers in America and in England. I soon returned to Antioch to finish my college course.

" In 1881 I graduated, and shortly after received a call from a large Church in Kessab, a town situated about thirty-six miles southwest of Antioch, near that ancient Roman road which used to run between the capital of Syria and Jerusalem. I accepted this responsible position, and now recalled the pamphlet which had been put into my hands three years before. I said to myself, ' Now, you are just fresh from the college, have no theological training whatever, neither books in that line. It will be a help to you to subscribe for that magazine.' So a friend wrote for me to Boston, and I received the *Homiletic Monthly* instead of the *Metropolitan Pulpit*—the same paper, I was told, with the name changed.

" From this time on a new world was opened before

my eyes.   My coming in contact with Western ideas
on our great religion, the ways in which the divine
truth was unfolded to the souls, altered my feelings,
and gave me a new inspiration.   Henceforth I had an
intense longing to hear those servants of the Lord
preach and speak to me, not through the medium of
the press, but face to face and soul to soul.   I finally
decided to go to the United States, to come in contact
with the men whose written words had so stirred me;
and to get my theological training in one of the sem-
inaries.

"Among many sermons I had read, I remembered
one with special pleasure, on I. Thess. v. 22—' Abstain
from all appearance of evil,' by Rev. Charles F. Deems,
D.D., Pastor of the Church of the Strangers, New
York City.   After reading the sermon I put in my
diary the names of the Pastor and his Church, with the
hope that God would some day open a way for me to
find the Church and its Pastor.

"On July 6, 1883, I left the port of Alexandretta, a
place near Tarsus, the birthplace of Paul, for New
York, where I arrived in the latter part of August.
My first work was to find out the Church of the
Strangers.   I inquired in one of the missionary rooms
at the Bible House, and a kind lady gave me the address.   I went out to locate the church (for it was
Saturday), so as to be on hand in good time for the
services in the morning.   Soon after breakfast next
day I hastened to the church.   It was time for Sunday School.   I sat on the bench with a happy heart,
yet with a strange feeling.   The Superintendent

came to me and kindly asked if I would like to be in a class. ' Certainly, sir,' said I, and the next moment I was one of the members of the Bible Class for Strangers.

" I remember still with great delight how I was overwhelmed with joy when they sang a hymn which I used to sing with my own people (I believe it begins with these words: ' Jerusalem Above'). This coincidence and the fact that I was in a place so long desired thrilled me exceedingly.

" Thus far I had not yet met the Pastor. I was expecting him to be in the Sunday School as a Superintendent and then as a teacher, according to the custom with us. I was disappointed, for I did not see him.*

" When school was over I hastened to the Church. I was cordially ushered into a pew, and at last the Pastor appeared in the pulpit. The sermon was on 1 Cor. ii. 2; the discourse emphasized two principal points, viz.: (*a*) that we must know more than anything else *Jesus Christ and Him crucified*, and (*b*) that the members of the Church must *preach* only Christ and Him crucified.

" I cannot tell how much I enjoyed the sermon, and how my heart was filled with joy ; for this was to me the realization of the longing of my heart, and of the hope which I had cherished while at home in the mountains of Antioch—the same mountains that

---

* He had probably been there and retired before the arrival of the stranger ; for the Pastor never fails to address the school when he is in town.   J. S. T.

once echoed the preaching of Paul, and that furnished the text for the immortal Epistles of that Apostle.

"After the regular service the Church had communion, and I too remained for that. I received the sacred emblems at the hands of the Pastor, who had no idea to whom he was ministering. At the conclusion of the services my Sunday School teacher introduced me to Dr. Deems, and the culmination of my happiness of that blessed day was the warm welcome I received from him. Learning that I desired to talk with him, the Pastor gave me his address, and invited me to call on him. During my stay in the city, which was a short one, I attended the Church as one of its members.

"This is the story of how I became acquainted with the Church of the Strangers. And I am ready always to acknowledge this, and gladly, too, that it was the kindness and affectionate welcome I had found in this house of God for strangers, and more especially the sympathy and love of Dr. Deems, that made my days of loneliness and sadness happy and blessed.

"May God Almighty prosper the Church of the Strangers in love, purity, and activity, and prolong the life of its blessed Pastor, the father of strangers, and bless abundantly his labors."

XIX.

What Then?

WHAT is to be the future of the Church of the Strangers? is a question that is often asked. Who can tell what is to be the future of anything? Men are seldom remembered by anything which they suppose will make them famous. Many a man has begun an enterprise that had in it the germ of something as different from itself as an oak is different from an acorn. Sometimes an institution does its full work and loses its institutional character in the diffused results of its existence. It becomes, in the language of the law, *functus officio ;* its office has been discharged in creating other causes. It may be so with the Church of the Strangers when its present Pastor has passed away. He has devoted the twenty best years of his life to this work. Some of the results may be summed up :—

1. Fourteen hundred and seventy-five persons have been enrolled in the Church membership. Of these seven hundred and forty were brought in on confession of faith. All these souls have enjoyed whatever good came out of the worship, the instruction, the general culture, the co-operative benevolent efforts and Christian intercourse of the whole body. Young men who are now active in Christian work were brought into the Church mere babes. They have

grown up in its atmosphere, and been moulded by
the character of its Pastor. Offshoots have appeared
in several directions, and, being a Church in which
there is much coming and going, its influence has
extended in every direction in which its members
have moved and wherever any of them are now settled. This the Church of the Strangers has not in
any singularity, but in common with every Church.
Some other Churches have undoubtedly done more,
and some less, in all these directions than the Church
of the Strangers; but this is to be taken into account
whenever we are striving to settle the question—
"What good will the Church have wrought, even if
it should at once become extinct?"

There is no probability, however, of its speedy ex-
tinction. A Church as firmly wrought together as is
this; situated in what is considered on all sides a
most unfortunate location; yet having one of the
largest memberships in the City of New York, must
have in it some compactness which will probably
cause it to live.

2. It might be difficult for a philosophical observer
to determine how much the existence of the Church
of the Strangers is due to the growing fraternal feeling among the sects, and how far the Church of the
Strangers has been an active factor in producing
these results. It seems to have been Providential that
the man who was raised up to be the Pastor of this
Church should have had so many qualifications for
uniting many elements apparently diverse. He was
born a Southerner and married a New York lady of

the best connections. His father was a Methodist minister. His religious education before going to college was under Protestant Episcopal auspices, and at college he came under pronounced Presbyterian influences. Before he was of age he was agent for the American Bible Society, which introduced him to the different denominations of Christians. Very early in life he was Professor in a State University. This also had a tendency to make him familiar with the best side of several Churches, and he had enjoyed further enlargement from European travel. And so he came into a position in which, without any trimming or catering to particular theological views, and preaching just along the lines on which he had always preached, he was acceptable to every denomination. His Church was really an Evangelical Alliance ecclesiasticized. Fourteen different denominations of Christians are represented among its communicants. It has demonstrated the practicability of Church union. It has never antagonized denominationalism ; but its Pastor, its officers, and its members have always spoken well of all the existing Churches ; and, while independent in itself, it has been in pleasant communion with them all. It has never professed itself a model on which every Church under all circumstances should be framed ; but it has shown the practicability of having Churches, under some circumstances, in which there were found sufficient bonds of union in the fundamentals of Christian faith and Christian practice. It has furnished a model for the kind of Church which *probably ought to be in every small town of not more than five or six thousand in-habitants.* It has done much by its very existence to assist in the efforts made to bring together in the unity of the spirit and in the bond of peace all who love our Lord Jesus Christ in sincerity.

3. The Church of the Strangers, under its present organization, may disappear from the institutions of the earth. Everything must die in order to be quickened. The Apostle calls attention to this in the case of seed. It is so in the case of men. Wherever a man has raised a party in philosophy, in politics, or in religion, that must be broken up if he has any principles worth disseminating.

4. The Church has had no small share in bringing about a better state of feeling between North and South. In an opening chapter it is related how Dr. Deems found the pulpit of New York uncomfortably plain-spoken about the South. The war had just closed, and the passions of that fierce struggle were not yet allayed. The words " With malice toward none, with charity for all " had, indeed, been spoken; but they had not yet been wrought into the thought and feeling of either the North or the South. All this was not strange, but it was unfortunate. Dr. Deems had the rare tact of preaching an energetic Gospel without giving offense to any human being that called himself by the name of Christ. He seemed to speak to the North as one who knew he was accountable to the South for every word uttered ; he spoke to the South as one who was willing to be responsible to the North for what he said anywhere. To appreciate the

difficulty of such a ministry, let one accustomed to speak or write much look carefully over his favorite illustrations, allusions, and sentiments, and see how they would sound to a Charleston audience, if he be a New Yorker, or to a New York audience, if he be a resident of Charleston. Every man has his prejudices. Dr. Deems doubtless had his ; but he sought out neutral ground and there planted his batteries, not against sections or creeds or parties, but against the common enemy of the race. It was very curious how the Union men of New York packed the church to hear this " rebel " preach ! Many of the sects hated one another right heartily, yet in the Church of the Strangers they came together to hear the Word of God, and were happy to be known as brethren. When Dr. Deems goes South, as he frequently does, to lecture and preach, he is thoroughly imbued with Northern modes of thought and speech ; yet all his discourses are without offense. And the strangest part of it all is that, while the Pastor of the Church of the Strangers has been thus the mediator between warring brethren, there has been no dissimulation, but simply a discreet silence on controverted subjects, and a wise cultivation of the good and generous elements in all men everywhere.

The following incident is related as illustrating the above statements :

After Dr. Deems had been conducting services for about a year in the chapel of the University, a gentleman who took very great interest in the movement asked him for the privilege of a call upon him by a gentleman residing in New York, who had come from Boston. The Doctor said he would be very happy to see any gentleman who would do him the honor to visit him.

" But," said his friend, " my friend connects his request for an interview with a singular, and perhaps, to you, unpleasant provision. He desires to call at the house when he will be perfectly sure not to meet any ' Southern Brigadiers.' He especially desires to avoid all Southern people."

" Why," said Dr. Deems, " does he not know that I am a Southerner?"

" Yes, he does ; he wishes to avoid Southern people in general, but wishes to see you in particular."

" Well," said the Doctor, " tell him to come on such a day at any hour, and if there happen to be any callers from the South, I will see that it shall be arranged to save him the offensive sight."

On the appointed day the gentleman called and sent up his card. Immediately upon entering the parlor the Doctor was struck with the sight of his visitor. It was a gentleman he had often seen so attentive and so devout at Church service.

He said to his visitor, "Your card tells me your name, after I have known your face for months intimately, and I have been told of your especial desire not to meet any one who comes from the South."

"Yes," said he ; "Doctor, I did make that a proviso. I am an intensely loyal man. I feel very bitterly toward the South. I cannot forgive the attempt to disrupt the Union."

"Then, why did you ever come to hear me preach when you knew that I was a Southerner, and had been in the South through the whole of the late unpleasantness?"

"Why," said the visitor, "I came because I hated you. I thought I would be able to detect in you something sinister and treasonable, and thus crush you. Now, for six months I have watched you closely. I have especially watched your prayers. No preacher that I ever knew before could hide his politics from me in his prayers. Those that I had been acquainted with invariably told the Lord in prayer, and thus told the audience, what their political bias was. But if the Lord knows your politics He must have learned them from your private prayers, for I have never heard a word uttered by you on your knees which might not have been spoken by any Christian man in America. You have done nothing but preach the Gospel, and lead the devotions of the people. And now I have come to say that I am ready to subscribe a thousand dollars toward building you a Church."

5. When the Church of the Strangers first commenced its work, there was but one Church in this whole city—an obscure Methodist Church—that advertised an invitation to "strangers." Before twenty years had passed, a large number of Churches had adopted the free-seat system. Almost every Church, even the most aristocratic and exclusive, became somewhat "Churches of the Stranger." It would be very difficult now to find a Church in the City of

New York in which a stranger would be ordered out of a pew into which he had inadvertently inserted himself; whereas, before that time, it would have been exceedingly difficult to find a Church, in which the pews were rented, where the stranger would not have been asked without much ceremony to vacate his seat. Perhaps when all the Churches in the great city have become Churches of the Stranger, the present organization bearing that name will pass away, and its whole work will have been accomplished.

6. In reply to the question, " What do you think will be the probable future of the Church of the Strangers? " Dr. Deems made this answer, which we are permitted to publish :—

"4th May, 1886.— The future of the Church of the Strangers gives me no concern whatever. There was a time when it did not exist, and probably there was no one who would not have been at that time more ready to predict the coming of such an institution than myself. I certainly never designed it ; I never intended to be at the head of a non-denominational Church, existing in the style of the Churches in the days of the Apostles. I am like a fly caught in the amber. I have endeavored to follow the leadings of Providence ; have forced nothing; have not been a beggar outside the Church nor a tyrant inside the Church : all men who know the circumstances should bear witness to the truth of that. I have simply done my duty as it arose ; and no one knows more than I do how poorly each duty has been discharged. So long as I live, and Providence does not open another door to me, I shall stay and do what I can in the Church of the Strangers. I should not hesitate to leave the Church of the Strangers to-morrow if I saw that I could probably do more good elsewhere. If I should die to-morrow, I should quietly leave the whole future of the Church of the Strangers in the hands of the Divine Master feeling that it was as safe as it was before I ever dreamed of it. It is His Church, not mine. I am willing for it this day, or this week, or ten years hence, to be dissolved. I have an abiding faith that it will stay where it is while it has work to do down in Mercer Street; that it will then be removed to some better field, or reappear in some other form or under other name, or give place to some better mode of work. The motto of the Church has been 'All for Jesus'; He will do what He will with His own. I am profoundly grateful to Him and to all those whom He has allowed or stimulated to help me in this blessed work by the space of twenty years. I am happy in my work, discontented with nothing but the defects in my own personal and pastoral life. As I grow older I trust that I shall not fossilize, and not try to prevent that flux of things which God has plainly ordained to be the method of motion and of progress in all the universe."

XX.

The Pastor's First Sermon.

THE desire has been expressed to have for preservation in this history the first sermon delivered by the Pastor in the Church of the Strangers. The first two Sundays in October, 1870, were occupied by opening exercises, which have been described in earlier pages. On the morning of Sunday, 16th of October, the Pastor took up his regular pulpit ministrations, and delivered a discourse which, when published, was entitled "Christianity Confronting Frivolous Skepticism." It resembles the other printed sermons of Dr. Deems, in merely giving the substance and showing the modes of thought of the preacher, but scarcely suggesting the vividness of his pulpit style. He is accustomed to use his notes merely as guides, making frequent dashes away from the prescribed line. Those who have heard him will perhaps supply, in a large measure, his manner of delivery.

THE TEXT : "I AM NOT MAD, MOST NOBLE FESTUS."—*Acts*, xxvi. 25.

[The sermon opened with an account of the events which brought the Apostle Paul face to face with Agrippa and Festus, together with a brief synopsis of Paul's statement of his case, which, for want of space, is omitted.]

When Paul reached the point of the resurrection of the dead, Festus—ignorant, frivolous, cold, and skeptical—cried out, in ridicule : "*Paul, thou art beside thyself;*" but, being a gentleman, and feeling how vile it would be to insult a prisoner in his power, he instantly and politely added : "much learning doth make thee mad." And Paul, full of power and enthusiasm, but most mannerly and refined, made the solemn reply of the text : "I am not mad, most noble Festus, but speak forth the words of truth and soberness." And, turning from the ignorant governor, he addressed to the royal voluptuary beside him an appeal so courtly, so reasonable, so powerful, that all present must have felt the falseness of the charge of Festus.

This does not seem to be the only occasion in which an aberration of intellect was imputed to Paul. There are several expressions in the Epistles (as in 2 Cor. v. 13) which imply that he was considered to be beside himself. But this imputation was not a peculiarity of Paul's case. Generally, the men of the world, those who study and pursue " the things which are seen," regard the men who gaze at " the things which are not seen " as crazed. The conduct of the latter is so contrary to all the opinions, principles, and modes of reasoning of the former, that they can be accounted for only on the supposition of mental derangement. And the fact is that somebody *is* crazy. If Festus, spending a life of frivolity and selfishness ; if Agrippa, wasting his powers in voluptuousness and licentiousness ; if Bernice, degrading her beauty to lust and incest —if these people were living *reasonably*, then Paul was an eminent fool. But if Paul, in abandoning the advantages of learning, rank, and influence; in breaking the dear and powerful bands of early associations ; in embarking all he was and all he had in the seemingly frail enterprise of this new religion; in forsaking all and following Christ, counting all but loss for Christ—if he was sane, then Festus, Bernice, and Agrippa were utterly mad. The dilemma presented itself clearly to Festus ; and so, to save himself, he cried : " Paul, thou art beside thyself." But Paul gave him the retort courteous in the reply, " *I* am not mad," and by the significance of his emphasis and his glance, said : " One of us *is* deranged, most certainly ; but, Festus, it is not *I*."

Just so have you who are unconverted frequently felt. You have seen devotion to Christ lead your friends away from frivolities, from the slavery of fashion, from selfish indulgences, from all the pleasures of " the lust of the flesh, the lust of the eye, and the pride of life ;" you have seen that devotion issue in a consecration of body, intellect, power, property, and life to the cause of Jesus ; and it has seemed to you amazing, and you have said : " These Christians are mad." And thus you have dismissed your conscience.

And you, dear Christian brethren, when you have seen the worldly forgetter of God go prospering in his way, and have been compelled to endure poverty and privation for the election you have made to follow Christ, have had a suspicion cross your minds, that perhaps your course was one of folly, if not of real madness ; and the very suspicion has been a momentary weakness. It certainly is true that, *if sinners be not crazy, then true Christians are mad.* But are Christians mad ? Does devotion to Jesus and hope of salvation from the hell of sin, through His merits and offices, argue a diseased intellect ? If so, where is the diseased spot in the spiritual constitution ?

Where is the madness ?

Let us specify :

1. He believes there is a God, Sovereign Governor as well as Almighty Maker of the Universe. He receives this proposition from intuition, or else he reaches it by logical processes. There *is* such a thing as intuition. Immediately, without intervention or aid of a

third idea or middle term, the mind perceives the agreement or disagreement of two ideas. In mathematics, a proposition so received is called an axiom. In morals, we speak of self-evident propositions. Suppose the Christian take the ground that he perceives *intuitively* the truth of this proposition: could you any more easily show that this arose from a diseased state of his intellect, than you could show that he is deranged when he takes the ground that he perceives by intuition that a whole is greater than any of its parts? Or suppose he have reached a conviction of the truth of the proposition of the existence of a personal God by logical processes, believing that His eternal power and Godhead are demonstrated by the things He hath made, would you not have as great difficulty in showing—not simply a fallacy in the reasoning, for that occasionally occurs with the sanest man, and is not now the question, but —that this conclusion, or the mode by which it was reached. demonstrated a *diseased* intellect? If you undertake this in regard to the Christian, you are to do the work so thoroughly as to show that not only he is crazy, but that, as well, all Jewish and pagan philosophers and poets, who have stood in princely pre-eminence in the Court of Thought, have been madmen; that all the leaders of mankind, those who in every other department of intellectual operation have been master-workmen, are here utterly at fault; and that the great majority of men in all ages have been deranged.

But from all other professing theists the Christian is distinguished by *feeling* as he *should* feel when this proposition is believed. If there be a God, He must be the moral ruler of the Universe; He must be the Father of our spirits. It is just here that Christianity comes in with its blessed offices of illumination and direction, and quickening of the moral sense. "Oh, yes, there is a God, certainly," says another man, and goes about his work or his pleasure as if God were nothing to him, as if He were not Moral Governor and Judge, and as if the man were no kinsman of God. The Christian has adoring reverence, and tender, child-like, filial regard for the loving All-Father. Say "God" to him, and it is as if you said "Mother" to an invalid child separated by leagues of sea from that one sweetest, dearest friend to whom it owes its life. Say "God" to him, and instantly you envelop his whole moral nature in a sense of the existence of a law that is holy, just, and good. He *feels* that there is a right and a wrong, that the right pleases and the wrong displeases THE *Father;* that the right is good and the wrong bad; that the right is life and the wrong is death. His loves and hates, all .his emotions, are under the shaping hand of this powerful belief. And so he is brought to love the pure, the beautiful, and the high, and to hate the filthy, the ugly, and the vile.

Now, is that healthy or otherwise? Mark, the question is not now whether there be a God, but whether, believing there is a God, a man should feel as a Christian feels. It is now a question con-

cerning the emotional part of man. Is it madness, when you believe that a certain man is your father, to feel filially toward him,
whether you be mistaken on the question of paternity or not?

A Christian is one who is striving to conform himself to a relation which he believes to exist between God and himself, being
impelled thereto by *feeling* as he ought to feel on faith in the existence of that relation. Does that prove an unhealthy state of *the
will?* Is it madness to *will* to do what you *feel* you ought to do,
because you *believe* that you ought to do it? That is the case of
the Christian as to God. Paul is *not* mad, most noble Festus !

2. A Christian believes that the " Father of Lights and of Spirits "—one of his synonyms for " God "—does give light to spirits,
divine illumination to the souls of men ; and that this is done
partly by a revelation which is in words, now printed, in a book
well known as the Bible, and partly by the unseen influence of His
Spirit upon man's spirit. Does that demonstrate mental alienation ?
Hold yourselves to the real question. It is not, is the Bible the
inspired Word of God, and if so, how and how far ? All parts of
that question might be answered variously, and yet a man be
mentally sane and intellectually consistent in believing the Bible to
be the Word of God, in a sense not applicable to any other known
book. The objector must show, not simply that there has been
some fallacy in the process by which a Christian reaches the conclusion that God *most probably* would reveal His will to man ; that
He would *most probably* do so as he believes it is done in the Bible ;
but he must show that none but a crazy man would accept such
premises of the Christian, or, from such premises, reach such con-
clusions. The burden of proof is on Festus, not on Paul. We
will not prove our sanity, Festus, but we challenge you to prove
our insanity. Show that it is madness to believe that the Father
will speak to His children ; that He will hear us crying in the
night and strike no light and speak no word and make no sound
to hush, to soothe, to help us ; that it is madness to believe that a
Father has a father's heart and bowels of compassion toward His
offspring, and an earnest wish to lead the wanderer back to the lost
home. You must show me that it is madness to believe that I
have a father, knowing my whereabouts and disposed to address
me a line of confidence and love ; or that this letter which I hold in
my hands, written in style so like all his authentic chirography
elsewhere, and full of such sentiments as befit his well-known
character, and telling me about myself as none but he, that hath
begotten me, and sudied me profoundly all my life long, *could* tell,
and, responding to all that my heart wants of my father ; that this
letter is a delusion and a nullity ; you must show *that*, or you
will never prove me deranged in my intellect for joining all Christians in believing in the divine authority of the Bible. And, Festus, before beginning this work, you must recollect that, when you
undertake to make good the allegation of mental derangement

against the intellect of the least developed and most illiterate Christian, you must be ready to make thorough work, and to demonstrate that also Bacon and Locke, also Newton and Boyle, also Shakespeare and Milton, also Washington and Bonaparte, and all other greatest masters in physical and metaphysical science, all other greatest builders of the loftiest rhyme, all other greatest governors of men and nations, in all the later centuries, have been diseased of mind, as well as Paul. And, Festus, this consider : that in traveling that long and heavy road, you must carry the weight of this fact, that, during the past five hundred years, no man has failed to recognize the Bible as the word of God who was not known and acknowledged to be of diseased intellect or deranged moral nature, whatever may have been the splendor of his intellectual endowments, as Voltaire, and Rousseau, and Paine. Paul is not mad, most noble Festus, because he believes that the Bible is God's word.

And, then, the real Christian feels as a man ought to feel, and acts as a man ought to act, who believes that he holds in his hands the very word of God, a revelation of His character, His will, and His plan for man's redemption. The accusation of madness is never brought by worldlings against the men who give merely the cold assent of their intellect to the dogma of the divine origin of the Bible ; it is leveled at those *who, believing it, feel and act accordingly.* Well, would it not be madness to do otherwise ? To believe that God has spoken to me and told me who and what He is ; that He has brought life to light, and immortality to light, showing me how to live and how to die, and how to prepare for the life beyond—and then to pay no more attention to the solemn utterances of the Infinite Spirit than to a gypsy's predictions or an infant's prattle—this were transcendent folly. Is it madness in the Christian to endeavor to live according to a directory he believes has come from heaven ? Is it madness to feel reverence for the tones and syllables of the great God ? Is there not a sublime consistency in Paul's surrender of the present for the future, of the temporal for the eternal ? Is there not an intellectual dignity in the quietude with which he bears the necessary and brief embarrassments of that surrender, in confident assurance of a final triumph ? Beside him, what drivelers do Festus and Agrippa appear !

I must beg you to keep in mind the point I am striving to make in this discourse. It is not to prove that there is a God, that the Bible is His word, that the Christian is logically correct in his views—all this I believe, but am not proving—nor am I striving to prove a negative *directly ;* all I hope to accomplish is to make you feel the silliness of those—of yourselves, if you do it—who make the grave charge of madness against Christians, when it is impossible to prove it, because all the serious probabilities are on the other side.

3. Keeping this in mind, let us consider the Christian's view of of himself, and examine the course of life founded on that belief.

(1.) He holds his sins up to the teachings of the Bible. Can
any sane man do that and not see "the exceeding sinfulness of
sin?" Upon that perception follows the intense hatred of sin. He
repents. He changes his mind. He once thought sin profitable
somehow, and he loved it. He now sees at the cross of Jesus
Christ, as you cannot elsewhere show him by any process known
to the laws of thought, how hideous a thing sin is. He sees that it
violates the harmony of the universe, and that thus each man's
every sin is an injustice to every other intelligent being in the universe, and thus indescribably offensive to the Holy Father of all
spirits. He now regards it as the violator of all the noblest sancti-
ties and all the most tender and sublime relationships of God's
wonderful world : and he hates it. He sees how, above all things,
it is his own greatest injury ; and he hates it. His repentance is
not a mere *change of mind* in his intellections, but it pervades *all*
his inner constitution. It rouses his emotions. He does not
simply regret the evil act. He *hates* it. It shames him. The remembrance thereof is grievous. He would hide the filthy thing
from God, from angels, and from men. Oh ! if he could but hide
it from himself ! And he ceases to do evil. Now, is that madness ?
If there be a God, and if he has created beings capable of character, there must be the possibility of sin. Having sinned, is it not
really the most healthful feeling to be poignantly sorry for the deed
of wrong and to hate it ? Is it not madness to go on as if you
were decent and virtuous and comfortable, when you have sinned ?
Look at these two sights.
There is a man hale and powerful in his appearance, tied to
another body. Go near and look at them. See, the body is dead !
The bonds which bind the living to the dead are of steel ; they
break not. But, behold ! The live man does not wish to have
them broken. He hugs and kisses and caresses the corpse. Oh
horrible ! The carcass has painted cheeks and polished teeth, but
its beauty is hideousness and its odor the exhalation of the charnel
house ! Oh, thrice horrible ! the wretched man pats and pets and
embraces this decaying body, inhales corruption, revels in putre-
faction, and is desperately enamored of the dead. He has lost love
of father and mother, of home and of manhood, in this fearful infat-
uation. He resents furiously all attempts to release him. He is in
love with death.
And there is another man. He too has a dead body bound to
his living person. And the bonds are strong. But see how he
struggles. He shuts his eyes to exclude from his vision the grin-
ning ghastliness ; he strives to lock up every sense that the hor-
ribleness of his companion may not fill him and kill him with
overpowering disgust. He pushes ; he struggles with the bonds
that make this unnatural union. He strains every muscle and
nerve for deliverance. The sweat rolls from him. The tears flow
down his cheeks. He pleads with man and fate, angels and God,

he appeals to the bowels of humanity and the heart of Deity to loose or annihilate him. He makes prayers to fire and lightning, to earthquake and storm for freedom. He beseeches death to make him dead with the dead, since such a life is bitterer than all destruction.

Which of these twain is the madman? The former has no emotions and behavior corresponding with his condition, the latter has; the former is Festus and the latter Paul; the former is you, the latter is your penitent neighbor.

(2.) When a man comes to know himself a sinner and to feel it, and to strive to keep from sin, does he not thereby acknowledge that he has committed offense against some one to whom he sustains relationship? Is not that God? Is it madness to seek forgiveness from a Being so powerful; or unmanly, when the offense is against all love? Is it madness to seek to be reconciled, when alienation is a disgrace and an injury, and when there is every reason to believe, that which we take to be God's Word teaches, that without reconciliation this alienation from God is to work in us an everlasting wrong and wretchedness? But how is a man to be reconciled to God? Paul felt, what you and I often feel, not that God is man's enemy, but that man is God's enemy; not that the Divine heart is enmity to man, but that "the carnal heart is enmity to God;" not that God has to be reconciled, but that man has to be reconciled. But he felt his natural helplessness, as every Christian man has done. Would God help him? It would seem that if He be "our Father" He will help us.

Paul looked all about for signs of God's work of reconciliation. He did not find it in nature, where God had established laws that often seem so frightfully inevitable. He did not discover it in providence, where the eyes of the wicked stand out with fatness while the righteous man perisheth and no man layeth it to heart. His thoughtful and logical mind still asked, "Where is God reconciling the world to Himself?" He made the discovery in Christ Jesus. He found, when a man purely and simply took Christ to be his wisdom, his righteousness, his sanctification, his redemption, that that man became reconciled to God and had a sense of forgiveness. *How* he could not tell. Nor could he tell *how* vitality was sustained by food. He found it was *so*. It was effectual in thousands of cases. As far as the human mind can discover, *it was God's Law in these premises*. At least no man could show that it was not. Nothing better offers. This plan succeeds. Is he a madman for using it? Is he a madman at being transported to find this deliverance from the body of death? Is he a madman for loving God in Jesus with supreme devotion? Is he a madman for standing before the Cross of Him he believes to be the propitiation for his sins, and for singing with trustful vehemence—

"My *God is reconciled*,
His pard'ning voice I hear;
He owns me for His *child*,
I can no longer fear,
With confidence I now draw nigh,
And Abba, Father, Abba, cry!"

(3.) And you see, dear brethren, when a man looks below his acts to the nature from which they spring, he discovers that not simply is the fruit bad, but the tree on which it grows, and that the tree is bad because its sap is bad. He has made the discovery that he is *naturally depraved*. There may be differences of opinion as to whether this depravity be partial or total, even among Christians; but is a man insane because he believes that by nature he is depraved? Your science teaches you that each man inherits the physical and intellectual qualities of his ancestors, as far back as they can be traced; that depravity of body runs down the current of the race; that inherited depravity of intellect is a proposition easily demonstrable. If he reason analogically to a probable depravity of soul, how are you to show him a madman? And if he perceive that bad things come out of his nature and reason thence to the depravity of that nature, how are you to prove him insane?

Once having reached that conviction, would he not be at least an imbecile if he should make no effort to purge his soul and to purify his whole nature? A Christian is one who, if not yet holy, is at least seeking holiness. The Bible method is described as submitting the unholy spirit of men to the influences of the Holy Spirit of God. *There is no other scientific method of becoming holy.* You purge matter with matter. You apply material substances to your material bodies to cleanse them inwardly and outwardly of material filth and obstructions. Did you ever know any physician to attempt to purge a fearfully obstructed biliary duct by reciting to his patient a transcendently beautiful poem, or any surgeon attempt to discuss a tumor by presenting to the intellect of his patient a concatenation of conclusive arguments? On the other hand you purge mind with mind. You bring intellect to bear on intellect, to dissipate mental crudities and strengthen mental weaknesses. Would not that teacher be regarded as insane who should poultice the head of his pupil for stupidity, administer pills to develop his logical powers, or rub him with liniments to quicken his poetical perceptions?

Matter to matter, mind to mind, spirit to spirit—that's God's obvious law. You administer physical remedies for physical ailments or weaknesses; you present facts to the understanding, truth to the reason, grandeur to the imagination, and beauty to the taste, in order to elevate and purify a man intellectually—and you are sane. The Christian does that and still finds his spirit corrupt, What must he do? All the materials known to pharmacy will not "purge his conscience from dead works." All the facts observed

and recorded, all the truths uttered and written, all the poetry ima-
gined or fancied, will not, cannot, make him holy and full of hope.
Some of the most corrupt men have been as handsome as Apollo,
and some of the most corrupt women have been as physically wholesome as Hebe ; some of the most corrupt men have reasoned like
Bacon and rhymed like Byron, and some of the most physically
healthful, and intellectually gifted women have been Aspasias.
How must a man become holy? That is the grand question. He
must submit his unholy spirit to a holy spirit. All that physical
and metaphysical researches ever discovered show that. Every
discovery in physics, in mind, in psychology for a thousand years
goes to make good the theological tenet of St. Paul.

Now where is that Holy Spirit to which my spirit must be submitted for my sanctification ? Certainly not in any other man, because every other man is in my spiritual predicament. It is outside the circle of humanity. It is in some other kind of creature,
or it is in God. The *only* spirit in the universe in regard to whom
all reason says that He must be immaculate, and not only uncor-
rupt but incorruptible, is God the Almighty. The Christian acts, as
every candid atheist even will admit he ought to act, under such
reasoning and with such conviction ; he submits his spirit, his
ghost, to the Holy Spirit, to the Holy Ghost of God. With such
strictness of analogical reasoning and such healthfulness of feeling, and with the visible, blessed effects, how can you, Festus, how
dare you, with your denials, your want of affirmations, your no-
faith, turn upon this honest man, this man with upturned face and
straight forward life, this man of power to endure and courage
to dare all that man or hero ought to venture or to do, how dare
you call *him* madman ? You weakling, dawdling in the lap of
luxury, how dare you call him mad who has discovered and is
wielding a power which is to shake the nations when you are a
handful of ungathered ashes? You almost cipher, to be unmen-
tioned in all the ages except as you are to be held up to the contempt of the generations as another instance of a pigmy in spirit
on an Alps of power—that chained prisoner has crushed you with
one gesture of his left arm ; that man in bonds has pilloried you on
your throne forever.

Dear Christian brethren, *ye* are not crazy. But, oh ! it were
madness in you to profess these high beliefs of Paul, and go living
like Festus—to say daily '' our Father,'' and walk the world with
the forlorn air of orphanage ; to accept the Bible as the word of God,
and let it have no more influence upon your life than so much
waste and worthless paper ; to profess yourselves sinners, and seek
no salvation ; to acknowledge Jesus, and yet not let Him save you ;
to confess the Holy Ghost, and yet quench the Spirit, and refuse to
be sanctified. It *is* insanity not to feel as you ought to feel to be in
accord with your belief. and it is madness to have your wills and
lives run violently across your convictions. Oh, be *all* Christ's !

Let your consecration be round, full, and entire! It will tear you from many a present pursuit. It will draw on you the charge of singularity, eccentricity, craziness, insanity, madness. But if a clear faith, a pure hope, and an ardent love be madness ; if it be madness to have the " fruit of the Spirit," which is "love, joy, peace, long-suffering, gentleness, goodness, faith, meekness, temperance"; if to live heroically and die peacefully be madness, then I say *be mad*, and let the Festuses and the fools be sane! Then madness is grandeur and glory, and sanity is insignificance and contempt ; then madness is light and rapture, and sanity is gloom and wretchedness. Then better, far better, be a good, strong, consistent, happy, triumphant, earth-conquering, heaven-winning madman, than to be a wicked, weak, wavering, miserable, cowardly philosopher, to whom life is all puzzle and death all terror.

The above sermon owes its preservation to Mr. Joseph J. Little, of the firm of Little, Rennie, & Co. (now J. J. Little & Co.), a member of the Church of the Strangers. Mr. Little undertook to publish, on his own account, all the sermons preached on the Sunday mornings of the first year of the occupancy of the present home of the Church. The plates are still in existence ; and from them new editions continue to be printed.

BOOKS BY MAIL

A SPECIALTY.

—o—

SEND TO US WHEN YOU

WANT A BOOK

Advertised or Mentioned in any Paper
and we will send it

POST PAID

On Receipt of Price.

—o—

Send your Address for Sample Copy of

BOOK RECORD.

—o—

Correspondence Solicited,
Liberal Discounts.
Send for Circulars.

—o—

FOREIGN PUBLICATIONS

Imported at Most Reasonable
Rates.

—o—

WILBUR B. KETCHAM,

PUBLISHER,

71 Bible House,   New York.

WORKS BY CHARLES F. DEEMS, D.D., LL.D.,

Pastor of the Church of the Strangers, New York.

CHRISTIAN THOUGHT.

This is a Bi-monthly, 80 pp., handsomely printed, containing the Lectures and Papers read before the American Institute of Christian Philosophy, and many other articles. Read the following opinions:

PRESIDENT PORTER: "So many able articles, some of them very able," JOSEPH COOK, Boston: "Many brilliant and powerful pages." PROF. SMITH, University of Virginia: "I had no idea the journal was so *uncommonly* excellent." REV. DR. WAYLAND: "The best Christian thought of the day." REV. DR. DRINK HOUSE: "There is no more worthy publication." REV. DR. EDWARDS: "Brimful of intensely interesting and instructive matter." $2.00 a year; Clergymen, $1.50. Specimen copy, 25 cents. Contents of Volumes 1, 2 and 3 sent on application.

THE HOME ALTAR.

An appeal in behalf of Family Worship, with Prayers and Hymns for the Family and a Calendar of Lessons from Scripture for every day in the year. New Edition. Cloth. 281 pages. Price 75 cents.

From the many notices the following are selected:

"This little volume we have read again and again, and cannot speak too well of it. There will be hardly any need of preaching on family prayers where it circulates."—BISHOP MCTYEIRE.

"It seems impossible to read it and continue delinquent in regard to the duty in question. The prayers are all catholic and scriptural."—REV., DR SUMMERS.

"The appeal contained in it for family worship is the most powerful and persuasive we have ever read, and it seems to us must be irresistible."—REV. W. H. HUNTER.

"It is one of the ablest essays on the subject we have ever read."—REV. DR CROOKS.

WHAT NOW ?

This is the title of a beautiful book intended to be a present to young ladies quitting school and entering life.

Whole classes in some of our leading institutions have received copies as presents on graduating. As a Christmas or Birthday present, or token of kind regard for a young lady, nothing is more appropriate. Cloth. 126 pages. Price 50 cts.

DR. DEEMS'S SERMONS.

Forty-eight discourses, comprising Sunday morning sermons, preached from the pulpit of the "Church of the Strangers," New York Cloth, 8vo, 304 pp., $1.50.

WEIGHTS AND WINGS.

We give the following as a specimen of the tone of all the notices of the press which we have seen:

"A very handsome volume, whose contents are well worthy of the faultless dress in which the publishers have sent them forth. No professing Christian who reads it thoroughly can remain in doubt as to whether his Church membership is a help or a hindrance to his pastor—a 'weight or a wing'—as he prosecutes his laborious and painfully responsible mission. The whole tendency of the book is to improve the relations of communicants to their pastors; and it would be remunerative to the latter to urge its circulation. There is a freshness and force about these forty five chapters which would never arouse the suspicion that the writer is the pastor of a large and popular city church, and at the same time the editor of one of the foremost magazines of the country."—*Southern Christian Advocate.* Cloth. 272 pages. Price $1.00.

EVOLUTION: A SCOTCH VERDICT.

This book contains the substance of the lecture delivered by Dr. Deems, at Chautauqua, before the German Theological School of Newark, and else where, with much added matter. It is the latest discussion of the question. 108 pages, paper cover, 20 cents.

THE GREATER BLESSEDNESS.

A new tract by Rev. Dr. Deems. Five cents.

* The above works sent postpaid to any address on receipt of price, or any book, no matter where published or advertised. Send for circulars.

WILBUR B. KETCHAM, Publisher, 71 Bible House, N. Y.

www.ingramcontent.com/pod-product-compliance
Lightning Source LLC
Chambersburg PA
CBHW020350030726
47496CB00007B/2079